MW00682548

The
Shanghai Noodle
Killing

To Sam,

Best wishes

Ted

Plaston

The
Shanghai Noodle
Killing

STORIES

Ted Plantos

Seraphim Editions

Copyright © 2000 Ted Plantos

All rights reserved. No part of this publication may be reproduced or transmitted in any form or by any means – electronic or mechanical, including photocopying, recording or any information storage and retrieval system – without written permission from the Publisher, except by a reviewer who wishes to quote brief passages for inclusion in a review.

Acknowledgements

Some of these stories have appeared in the following publications and anthologies: *Exhibit B, Love and Hunger* (Mercury Press, 1990), *Paragraph, Great Canadian Murder and Mystery Stories* (Quarry Press, 1992), *Dandelion, lichen,* and *The Prairie Journal of Canadian Literature*.

Published in 2000 by
Seraphim Editions
970 Queen Street East
P.O. Box 98174
Toronto, Ontario
Canada M4M 1J0

The publisher gratefully acknowledges the financial assistance of the Canada Council for the Arts.

THE CANADA COUNCIL   LE CONSEIL DES ARTS
FOR THE ARTS   DU CANADA
SINCE 1957   DEPUIS 1957

Canadian Cataloguing in Publication Data

Plantos, Ted, 1943 –
    The Shanghai noodle killing: stories

ISBN 0-9699639-7-1

    1. Title.
PS8581.L34S52 2000   C811'.54   C00-900922-1
PR9199.3.P54S52 2000

Cover photo: Paul Sanderson
Author's photo: May Plantos
Design: Perkolator {Kommunikation}

Printed and bound in Canada

This is for Cliff Kennedy, who showed me where the
imagination could take a story.

Special thanks to Carol for all she gave to these stories, and to
Maureen and Allan for believing in this work.

I gratefully acknowledge Lloyd Cully's contribution to the
story "Ragtown", which grew out of conversations we had
about "our" Cabbagetown and its true historical boundaries.

Contents

The Shanghai Noodle Killing

H E DIED as he had lived, with his face in a bowl of noodles. This was not written into Ben Lee's obituary. Only the standard words applied: *A good father to five children. Lily Lee's beloved husband.* You understand. Nobody would have believed it. They'd have thought it was made up by someone who trifles with honesty, someone with a sordid sense of humour. Nobody dies with his face in a bowl of noodles. In a bowl of pasta done *al dente*, yes ... with blood mixing into oregano-seasoned tomato sauce, yes. But at Queen's Noodle House on Queen Street, who could predict it?

"Shanghai noodle ... the thick one," Lo told Elizabeth, who took notes for a story in the Gazette, a Chinese community paper.

"He liked them best, did he?"

"Ben very particular how noodle cooked. A few minute before the shooting, he complain they too chewy."

Elizabeth thought this stuff about the noodles would have plenty of human interest. "He was a perfectionist about how they were cooked," she said, and wrote it down when Lo nodded.

Lo was under the table when the gunmen opened fire. He tried to warn his friend. But you have to eat at Queen's Noodle House to understand that bedlam and not noodles or sizzling pork or anything on the menu or written in Chinese on the walls is the order of the day. There are thirty-five tables and each is surrounded by voracious stomachs and teeth that mash down into steaming plates of flesh and greens with chopsticks clicking, tongues salivating … and under the din there is a murmur, a low growl, if you will, that issues from the intestines of the eaters. Close your eyes and you are transported to Hong Kong. Open them in the mist of hot and sour soup and you see faces shifting like 144 mah-jong tiles. In the mystifying sweat of the moment, laced with oyster sauce, hunger is an addiction you can afford at these prices.

Lo explained. "I shout to Ben when I see those hoodlum come through door … Duck, Ben."

"Did he hear you?"

"Yes."

"What did he say?"

"He say, 'You order duck?' They his last word. 'You order duck?' Then the noise. It deafen me. People screaming, little children shrieking. I stay down, my head on the floor until police come. Then I get up, see Ben's face in the bowl. Blood all over. Ben's eyes open. But Ben dead."

Elizabeth puzzled over how she could work these lurid details into her story without offending anyone. This was her first gangland slaying. All the other stories were about natural deaths. He died in his sleep. She succumbed to a stroke. The kind of deaths you come to expect. Elizabeth had never heard about anyone being gunned down while eating a bowl of Shanghai noodles. She knew the editor would say 'Change this … change that …' until it sounded nothing like the way Ben Lee actually died on that Saturday afternoon in Queen's Noodle House. But how could the editor blame her? She was assigned to interview this man, Lo, because he and Ben were good friends. Didn't she ask innocuous questions? The kind she was expected to ask? Was it Elizabeth's fault that Lo wanted her to know all the sordid particulars?

"Ben owe money to wrong people," Lo told her.

Elizabeth tensed, anticipating the worst. She hoped that Ben Lee was not involved in narcotics, and that he owed money to a financial institution. Anything but narcotics. How could she write in her story that Mr. Ben Lee had a drug addiction?

"Gambling," Lo said.

Elizabeth sighed in relief. Gambling is not as bad as drugs. She would have to change Lo's words though. She would have to distort. Lie. Her story could explain that Mr. Ben Lee was a speculator. He was dining with a business associate, Mr. Lo Chen, at a downtown restaurant when he was cut down … no, slain by a gang that had tried to wrongfully extort money from him. She didn't have to mention the noodles – although it might lighten the story for the readers. Elizabeth believed her readers came first. If you can't be explicit about the truth, offer human interest – at least.

"Gambling his big problem," Lo continued.

Elizabeth thought for a moment before writing: *Mr. Lee was dedicated to his business.*

"Gambling like drug for Ben."

Elizabeth wrote: *When Mr. Lee was not at home with his family, or working at his business, he enjoyed recreational games of chance with his friends.*

"Ben was marked man," Lo explained. "I warn him, don't go to Queen Noodle. The mob know he love noodle. Too bad his last meal chewy."

This comment challenged Elizabeth's inventiveness. She tried: *Mr. Lee was known to frequent this restaurant because of its excellent noodles. With his final breath he courageously defied the criminals who would steal money from an honest citizen.*

"His family suffer because he gamble."

Elizabeth would have to lie: *Mr. Lee's family had supported him through some recent business difficulties.*

"He take money for his children education. Gamble it. No good."

Elizabeth stopped writing. She knew how hard her parents had worked so she might have an education. She believed no decent parent would gamble with his or her children's future. "Is this true?" she asked.

"It is tragic truth about Mr. Ben Lee. I am sad for him. Sad for his family."

Elizabeth believed Lo, who seemed like a sincere man. She had heard about people like Ben Lee. She too was sad. The true story could never be written. The censors would kill it. Perhaps the censors are also responsible. Who would a lie protect? The family, or the people who are afraid of the truth being exposed? Elizabeth didn't know, and she wanted to. She decided to ask Lo. "Do you want me to write the true story?"

Lo laughed. "True story?"

"What you have told me about Mr. Lee —"

"What I say about Ben Lee are the rumour, lie and shameful gossip you'll hear from other people."

Elizabeth could not believe that a friend of the deceased would be so cruel as to repeat these rumours. He had taken advantage of her, and lied to her. "You were his friend. How could you act as if these lies were true?"

"Why wouldn't I?"

"No, you answer my question first."

Lo explained. "Ben owed me money. Lots of money. What's truth or lie matter no more. We meet at Queen Noodle to discuss payment he miss."

"Why are you telling me this? I could expose you."

Lo leaned forward and whispered. "But you won't."

Lo was right. The editor would laugh her out of the office. It would never see print. But the gossip, and exaggeration? That's another story. Elizabeth didn't know what to believe. Lo saw to that.

Abby's Window

CRAIG SITS up in bed, rubs the sleep from his eyes and opens the curtains. A big snowfall last night. Few signs of life under the avalanche. A dog, up to its belly in the stuff, crosses the road. A woman on the second floor of the house across the street looks out her window, then closes the curtains. A man pushes open his front door against a mound of snow.

Craig stretches to loosen the kinks in his body. Upstairs, someone has turned on a radio and is listening to a weather report. Craig hears a kettle whistling, footsteps creaking on the stairs, and someone coughing. He opens his door a crack and peeks out into the hall at the tall man who lives on the second floor. Their eyes meet and Craig says, "Good morning."

The man nods, says, "Morning," and opens the front door. Snow flies into his face. He closes the door and walks back upstairs, coughing.

Craig steps out into the hall in his longjohns and looks up the stairs at the man. "I'll shovel the snow before you leave for work," he tells him.

The man mumbles something that sounds like "Thanks."

After a breakfast of tea and toast, Craig puts on his boots, coat and a purple toque and hauls the shovel and a bag of salt out of the closet. He steps outside, drops the bag onto the porch and starts shoveling.

Abby, the old woman next door, lifts her window and peeks out. "Oh, my God!"

Craig turns. "God has nothing to do with it, Abby. It's strictly the weatherman's fault," he says as he bends for another shovelful.

"Nobody said nothing about snow," she complains.

"Nobody tells us anything, Abby." Abby's cat squeezes between her and the window frame and looks out. She strokes the fluffy, grey longhair, looks into its big yellow eyes and says, "You don't wanna go out in that weather, Misty."

Craig takes a breather after shoveling the steps and walkway. He shields his eyes from the sun and turns to Abby's window. "It's actually quite mild out."

Craig tackles the sidewalk next, heaving snow over his shoulder onto the road. The man from upstairs opens the door and steps outside, holding a lunch pail. He stands on the porch for a moment and coughs into his hand before walking down the steps. He passes Craig, who says, "You're a brave man going to work on a day like this. Those streetcars won't be moving any too fast this morning." Craig rests his hands on the shovel and watches the man walk up the street. "He doesn't look well this morning, Abby. I heard him coughing through the night. His room is just above mine. He woke me up a few times. You know, he has that hacking cough that doesn't sound right."

"I hear the flu bug is going around," Abby says.

Craig finishes shoveling. "You think it's the flu he has?"

Abby reaches into her tobacco tin to roll a cigarette. "It's going around. My nephew is down with it. He's the one that works in the bank out in Mississauga."

"Maybe he shouldn't have gone to work with that hacking cough of his."

"He's got a temp job, don't he?" Abby asks.

"I'm not sure. He keeps to himself."

"Well, if he's temp, he can't call in sick or nothing, or he don't get paid."

Craig sighs. "It'll take more than a snowfall to stop him from working."

Abby nods and lights her hand-rolled cigarette. "He's a steady worker, and he don't bother nobody."

Craig takes the shovel back up to the porch and leans it against the wall. "Quietest tenant in the house. When he isn't working, he just sits in his room drinking beer and watching TV. Not a peep out of him."

The cat stretches and rubs itself against the side of Abby's head. "He drinks ... but who don't!"

"Just about everybody on this street drinks, Abby. How would we understand them otherwise?"

"I got a tenant on the third floor," she says. "He don't touch a drop. He's a student. Anyway, I go in his room one day when he's out, and there's books everywhere. On the bed and floor and all over the table."

Craig leans against the porch railing and turns to Abby. "You actually go inside your tenants' rooms when they're out? Shame on you, Abby!"

"Shhh," Abby says, and continues. "They're not ordinary books like what normal people read. No, they're these big heavy grey and black books that smell mouldy and got small print in them."

"Oh, I think I've seen·him. A rather grim-looking fellow."

Abby nods. "He's always got a frown on his face and he never smiles. Don't matter if you're pleasant to him or not. He don't smile – and when he talks, it's real slow like he's figuring out what word should go next. He speaks one word at a time like it's a real pain for him to talk, and he keeps his door closed all the time. My other tenants, they leave their doors open and visit each other to talk or drink beer. But not him. He don't like visitors. He never has nobody up to his room. He's so quiet, it's scary. No sir, I don't trust nobody who don't drink."

"Why did you rent the room to him?"

Abby shivers. "I didn't know what he was like. He scares me."

"I'm sure he's just some harmless intellectual," Craig says.

"Speaking of scary, I been seeing the inspector on the street a lot lately."

"Who?"

"Bernie I think his name is."

"Bernie retired last spring, so he's no longer an inspector. But his daughter and son-in-law bought a rooming house down the street. They live there with their two kids."

"A boy and a girl?"

"Yeah, Cory and Jessica."

"There aren't many kids on this street so you notice any new ones."

"Bernie visits them a lot and he's also friends with that fellow who raises pigeons over on Ontario Street."

Abby laughs. "You mean Gordy."

"Yeah, I think that's the name. Do you know him?"

"Sure, Gordy used to live here. He was a good tenant, but he had this crazy friend called Spud. Spud would stand outside here all hours of night pounding on the door and shouting up at Gordy's window. I don't think he's all there. Finally, I told Gordy if his friend came by again, he'd have to move. Gordy was the kind of person he wouldn't say nothing to hurt Spud's feelings. So he just moved."

"You're a mean old landlady, Abby."

"Hi, Freddie!" Abby shouts.

Craig turns to see the old man limping up the street, bent over.

"Good morning, Missus," Freddie says, then nods toward Craig.

"Watch your step, Freddie," Craig says. "I still have to put salt down."

"What's on special today?" Abby asks.

Freddie stops and looks up at her window. "Corned beef and cabbage."

"What's the soup of the day?" she continues.

"Navy bean."

Abby smiles. "Corned beef and cabbage and navy bean soup. That's a hearty meal for a day like this. That'll stick to your bones."

"Is there turnip in the corned beef and cabbage?" Craig asks.

"Ah, yes, turnip," Freddie says and continues up the street.

"There's someone else who don't let the weather get him down," Abby says as Craig fills his shovel with salt.

"How long has Freddie been working at the Confederation Grill?"

Abby turns away from the window. "Wait a minute."

Craig finishes salting the walks.

Abby crooks her finger at him. "Come over here," she whispers.

Craig climbs over the railing onto her porch and she hands him a plastic cup.

"Rye," she says, winking. "Sorry, I got no coke or ginger ale for mix."

"I have some coke in my fridge," Craig tells her. "I'll go —"

Abby taps her cup against his. "Never mind. We'll drink it straight up. That'll knock the chill from our bones."

Craig swallows his rye and scowls. He hands the cup back to Abby, who reaches around Misty to pour another for him.

Craig lifts the cup to sip. "Ah, I love this fire water."

Abby lights up another hand-rolled cigarette, spits out some tobacco bits and says, "Now what was it you asked about Freddie?"

Craig finishes the rye, sets the cup down on the ledge and tries to remember. "Oh yeah, I wanted to know how long he's been working at the Confederation Grill."

Abby puffs on her cigarette and ponders. "Since it opened ... I think. Oh, that goes back a long time. I think Freddie started the business with his brother when they came over from Greece in the early 1950's. The brother died and he took it over until he had that bad fall what injured his back."

"What fall?"

"Freddie was up on a ladder doing repairs on his ceiling when the ladder gave out from under him. That's the story I heard. He injured his spine. They closed the Grill a few days, then his daughter and son-in-law took it over."

"Steve and Mary!"

"Yeah, Steve and Mary. And now their son, Benny, Freddie's grandson ... he works there too."

"I think Freddie enjoys waiting on tables," Craig says.

Abby nods. "How many old men you know works fifty hours a week?"

Craig hands the cup to Abby. "I don't know anybody who works that many hours a week."

"The Greeks are solid people. They come to Canada, work hard and never complain."

"I worked for a Greek once," Craig says. "It was a little restaurant downtown in the business district. I waited on tables, washed floors and windows, made toast and sodas and delivered coffees to the office buildings. He paid me minimum wage, but threw in lunch and dinner."

"Did you like the job?"

"I stuck it out for a few months – but, you see, I was working five and a half days a week. That took out my Friday nights while everyone else partied – and I was dog-tired by Saturday afternoon when he closed. Also, I felt a little embarrassed about him having to show me how to mop a floor."

"But you mop floors now."

"Oh, sure! I mop floors, shovel walks, wash windows, keep peace in the house and do a little plumbing for Mr. Lin. I do everything but collect the rent."

Abby pours the last of her rye into the two cups. "He's a good man, Mr. Lin."

"Often, when Mr. Lin drops by, his wife sends food over for me. One day she came by and showed me how to use chopsticks.

'Better than fork,' she tells me. 'Oh yeah, try eating mashed potatoes with them,' I tell her. She didn't understand, but her husband
explained in Chinese, and she thought that was funny."

Abby finishes her rye. "What's your plans this morning?"

Craig hands Abby his empty cup. "There's a tap leaking in the
kitchen upstairs. I promised Old Bill I'd fix it for him today. Why'd
you ask?"

Abby whispers. "I was wondering maybe if … if you'd run me
an errand."

"The liquor store?" Craig asks in a whisper.

"Just a little bottle … a Mickey Mouse, you know. That's all what
I can afford. I'm expecting my pension cheque today, but I don't
know if it'll get here in this weather."

Abby removes some folded bills from her tobacco tin, but Craig
brushes her hand aside. "You keep your money. I've been sipping at
your window a lot lately. I figure I owe you. It's on me, Abby."

"You're a dear boy," Abby says as she tucks the bills back into
her tobacco tin.

Craig climbs over the railing onto his porch just as the door
opens and Old Bill pokes his wrinkled, pink dome outside.

"You're awfully anxious about that tap, Bill. I told you I'd fix it
today."

"Tap break," Old Bill says.

"What!" Craig shouts.

"Tap break! Water all over, Craig. Gushing!"

Craig squeezes past Old Bill and bolts up the stairs.

"What happened?" Abby asks.

"Oh, it's you, Abby. The tap break when I'm pour water for
make tea. Awful —"

"That's terrible. I guess Craig will be working on that all morning," Abby sighs as she puts the lid on her tobacco tin.

"But Craig fix it. No sweat. I go inside now … maybe help
Craig."

"You go inside before you freeze, Bill," Abby says as she lowers
her window. Inside her dark room, she turns on her TV and

watches a re-run of *The Honeymooners*. Misty curls up next to her on the sofa. She falls asleep and wakes an hour later with someone tapping on her window.

"Abby," someone calls, and she recognizes Old Bill's voice.

She opens the window and is handed a bag. "What's this?"

"Craig tell me get you Mickey Mouse," he explains.

Abby takes the bottle from the bag and smiles. "Bill, want to have a drink with me? I don't like drinking alone. It don't seem right."

"No thank you, Abby. Craig say come back right away to help him. I better go."

Abby closes her window, draws the curtain and limps to the kitchen to get a glass.

Pigeon Man

A T DAWN, high winds blast snow across the ragged rooftops. Towering high-rises to the east pale to fragile shadows in the tempest. The frazzled edges of neglected streets and back lanes soften under puffy mounds, and the old factories look almost magical – their sooty brick glistening from fresh flakes, and a glaze of frost on the bleak windows.

Gordy zippers up his coat and opens the creaking attic door to the roof. A gust of wind almost knocks him back inside. Gordy pushes his boots down into the snow and steadies himself as he makes his way cautiously to the edge of the roof where he looks down between buildings. "Rags, you all right?" he shouts at the pigeon nestled on the air conditioner outside the second-floor window of his room. Gordy smiles when the bird shakes a spray of snow from its wings and glances up at him. "You stubborn old bugger, why don't you hunker down in the loft with the others?"

DORIS SITS at the kitchen table and pours steaming black tea into her mug. Sipping slowly from her cup, she draws back the curtain and squints into the storm. "There's a man out on the roof across the lane there," Doris says.

Eileen glances out over Doris's shoulder. "Oh, that's the Pigeon Man."

Doris's mouth curls in disgust. "Pigeons! Echh, flying rats."

GORDY HEARS the cooing birds, and their happy sounds warm him inside. The loft he had built in the summer for the local pigeons now looks like an igloo. He brushes the snow off the roof with wide sweeps of his arm. His pets will be hungry.

"There's hot tea in the pot," Eileen says.

Doris puts her palm against the pot and draws it back quickly. "Oh, yeah, it's hot all right. I'm gonna make some toast. Want some, honey?"

"What's that ... it looks like a hut on that roof," Doris says, still staring out the window.

Eileen picks away some green mould from the bread and drops two slices into the toaster. "It's a loft. It's where he keeps his pigeons. I heard he's got perches and baths and rooms in there. It's quite the little production I understand."

"Pigeons carry disease, you know."

Eileen shrugs. "I've lived among pigeons all my life. Growing up in the city, they were the only wildlife I was familiar with. Pigeons don't cause any harm."

"That's not what I heard. But I was raised in a small town, so we never saw much of them. Pigeons are one of the things I don't like about the city. They just drone on with the traffic and general clamour in the streets. Pigeons typify the chaos of urban life."

"But that's what I like most about pigeons," Eileen says. "They are lawless, and humans are powerless to do anything about them. I often think the city belongs to pigeons."

"You give them too much credit. Pigeons are dumb."

Eileen smiles. "Yeah, so dumb they probably think that humans built churches, banks and courthouses just for them to nest and shit on."

GORDY UNLATCHES the door to the loft and stoops to squeeze himself inside, his coat pockets bulging from bags of seed and food scraps. He doesn't like leaving food out overnight for his birds because it might go bad. So he brings them fresh seed and scraps of vegetables every day – more in the winter when they need to bulk up. Gordy can't afford commercial seeds, so all through the spring and summer months, he had picked and gathered seeds from the weeds that had flourished in the back lanes and alleyways. Early last spring, he had set up a feeder outside the kitchen window, and its popularity surprised him. Gordy noticed that the birds preferred to eat in the early mornings and late afternoons. The other tenants who used the common kitchen didn't seem to mind the birds, and some even contributed scraps of food. Then a friend suggested to Gordy that he build a loft on the roof. Gordy laughed at the idea until the birds started nesting on the ledges and air-conditioners of the rooming house as if it were a cliff, and flocking in greater numbers to the roof whenever he put out scraps of food.

Rags, one of the first pigeons to set up lodging on the building, chose the top of the air-conditioner outside Gordy's room. Every morning, Gordy woke to the sound of Rags cooing. He was partial to the bedraggled slate-grey bird that always flew alone and stayed apart from the others at feeding time.

Fortunately, Gordy's landlord also liked pigeons and gave him permission to build the loft on the roof. When he completed the loft, Gordy's efforts at coaxing Rags to take up residence there were in vain. The bird was an independent spirit.

EILEEN SITS down at the table and spreads margarine evenly over her toast. "I don't even know his name. We just call him the Pigeon Man. The kids downstairs are fascinated by him and his pigeons. Cory and Jessica like to come up here to the third floor where they get a clear view of the goings on. They even bring binoculars. I get a kick out of their reactions."

"How old are they?"

"Cory's ten and Jessica's eight. They're really bright kids, and funny too. I split my sides listening to them."

GORDY'S BOOTS crunch down into the kitty litter on the floor of the loft. It is dry inside from the insulation and elevated floor. Some younger birds flock to him and he feeds them bits of lettuce from his hand. The older ones remain on their perches at the rear of the loft, secure in the knowledge they will be fed according to routine. He is pleased to know that his birds trust him.

Gordy has names for all of his pigeons, but some of the older ones leave and new ones arrive, making it difficult to kee͏ The younger ones who were hatched in the loft are ͏ always return after a flight. Gordy grew up in the cit͏ used to pigeons, but had never given them much th͏ bird was indistinguishable from the other, he thou͏ same ones kept returning to the roof, and he r͏ had a distinct personality that suggested a name͏

"I bet it's the kids at the door now," Eileen sa͏ last bit of toast into her tea.

"You stay put, I'll get the door," Doris says.

Cory and Jessica, rarely at a loss for word͏   t with the͏ binoculars and glance at each other while a st͏   ͏ smiles down at them.

Doris breaks the silence. "You must be C͏ and Jessica. I'm Eileen's friend, Doris."

Jessica sighs. "Did Eileen tell you all about us?"

"Only the good stuff."

"C'mon in, kids," Eileen shouts.

Cory and Jessica's faces brighten at the sound of Eileen's voice.

"The Pigeon Man just went into his loft to feed his birds," Doris tells them as Eileen stands behind her, massaging her neck.

Jessica glances at the women and says, "Are you lovers?"

Cory nudges his sister. "It's not polite to ask personal questions."

"That's all right," Doris says. "Eileen and I were close friends for a long time before we decided to live together. We love each other just like your dad and mom."

"Mom and Dad don't always love each other," Jessica tells her. "Sometimes they hate each other. They swear and say bad words."

"Well, so do we. Eileen and I get mad as hell at each other sometimes. Don't we, Eileen?"

"Adults are like that," Cory says as he parks himself at the window and adjusts his binoculars. "When I grow up, I'm gonna be like the Pigeon Man. He has no friends except pigeons – ."

"He has Spud," Jessica says. "The Pigeon Man's best friend's name is Spud."

"Who's Spud?" Doris asks.

Eileen laughs. "I shouldn't laugh, but Spud is –"

"Spud is a half-wit," Jessica says.

"Jessica," Cory cautions her, "don't call people bad names."

Jessica squeezes into the corner next to her brother at the window. "Well… everyone calls him that."

GORDY IS ON his hands and knees at the feeder when he hears the roof door slam shut and a voice calling him. "Gord … Gord … "

"I'm in the loft, Spud," he shouts.

Spud draws back the door and pokes his head inside. "Gord, I brung you some seeds what Mrs. Reilly gave me. She say give them seeds to Gord for him to feed his birds with. So I do that. Ain't I smart for that?"

Gordy takes the bag from Spud. "Of course you are. You're the smartest friend I have."

"But I'm your only friend."

"Then that makes me smart too."

"Can I come in the loft? Huh, Gord!"

"We both can't fit in here, Spud. So you best be on your way."

"Aw, Gord, can't I come inside which you and the pigeons?"

"There's some babies here who just hatched, and the mother is feeding them. She's very touchy when she's feeding her babies."

"What she feeding 'em?"

"Pigeon milk."

"Do she feed 'em from her beak, Gord?"

"Yeah, from the food stuff she brings up from her stomach."

"Gord, I said I'd scrape the loft clean for you. I'll clean up all the pigeon poop. Every last bit."

"I just scraped yesterday, but I promise to let you scrape next week."

"That's a promise. You always keep your promise, don't you?"

"No, not always, Spud. But I try."

"Yeah, you'll try, Gord."

"And you won't forget to remind me, will you?"

"I'll keep asking until you remember so you won't forget, Gord."

JESSICA LOOKS up from her binoculars and points out the window. "Look, there's Spud."

Cory adjusts the focus on his binoculars. "How do you know it's Spud?"

"Coz."

"Coz why?"

"Coz he's scratching his bum."

"A lot of people do that. Don't you scratch yours?"

"Yeah … so … "

"So a lot of people do it. Not just Spud."

"Jessica's right," Eileen says. "Spud scratches his bum a lot. He went to the store for me once when I was sick. Mrs. Reilly sent him over because he does errands for her. Spud stood inside the door here talking to me for about ten minutes, and he kept reaching back to scratch his bum. It gave me the creeps."

Doris crouches next to Jessica. "Honey, you're probably right about Spud. But maybe he can't help himself, and it would hurt his feelings to hear people say it."

"How come your teeth are yellow?" Jessica asks.

Doris covers her mouth with her hand. "Well, I haven't brushed them yet this morning."

ROMPIN RONNIE nestles on Gordy's shoulder and coos. Gordy brushes his face against the bird's silver-backed plumage, and Rompin Ronnie pecks at him affectionately. They share each other's warmth until Trixie flaps down from her nest and lands on his outstretched arm. "Trixie, don't you have some eggs to incubate?" Gordy glances up at the nest in the corner of the loft to see Big Daddy taking his turn on the two white eggs, his shiny feathers puffing up with pride as he settles in for a morning's nesting. "Ah, honey, you look all feathered out." Gordy says as Trixie, with head bobbing, wobbles up his arm and perches on his shoulder, competing with Rompin Ronnie for attention. He rubs her tiny head with the tip of his finger, and he can feel Rompin Ronnie's feathers ruffling against his neck. Gordy hears a flock landing on the roof, and he steps outside with Rompin Ronnie and Trixie on his shoulders.

"Jessica, look," Cory says. "The Pigeon Man just came out of the loft."

Jessica turns back to the window and looks through her binoculars. "He has two pigeons on his shoulders. And there's a bunch of other birds there too."

"Gramps says he knows the Pigeon Man."

"Yeah, Gramps said he'd take us to meet him."

GORDY STANDS at the door of the loft and glares down at a scruffy pigeon and his checkered pals. "Ok, Punkass, you and your hoodlum friends are not allowed in this loft. We have babies in here, and Trixie and Big Daddy are hatching some eggs. We don't need your kind upsetting them."

"Gramps," Jessica chirps as she runs to greet the elderly man. Cory follows Jessica and hugs his grandfather.

"Bernie, I'd like you to meet my friend, Doris," Eileen says.

Doris smiles up from the table where she sits and nods toward the window. "Hi, Bernie, Cory and Jessica are tuned into the bird channel here."

"Yes, I promised I'd introduce them to Gordon ... otherwise known as the Pigeon Man."

"Jessica says you know him," Eileen says.

"Oh, yes, I coached Gordon in hockey when he was a boy. He got in with a bad crowd later on and had a few scrapes with the law. When his marriage broke up, he broke up too. But Gordon was always a gentle boy. Perhaps too gentle for the world he was raised in."

Doris nods. "So it broke him."

Bernie smiles. "I think he's happy with his pigeons."

"I hope for his sake the Health Department is too," Doris says.

"I'm a retired health inspector, Doris. I've been working with Gordon on meeting all of the regulations. It hasn't been easy because he's such a maverick. I advised him to build the loft when he started feeding pigeons, and he was attracting birds from all over the neighbourhood."

"Actually, I've noticed fewer pigeons hanging around since he built the loft," Eileen remarks.

"That's right. Gordon has his own family of birds, and those are the only ones he feeds and cares for."

Punkass and his gang circle Gordy. He can feel Rompin Ronnie shaking while Trixie presses herself against his neck. "Calm down, Rompin Ronnie. And, Trixie, don't you worry. Punkass and his friends don't scare us."

GORDY HEARS wings overhead and looks up at Rags descending toward Punkass. Rompin Ronnie flies off from his shoulder and Trixie clings, her heart racing. Rags lands next to Punkass and sends up a spray of snow. The two birds flail against each other, their wings beating in a flurry of feathers.

A door slams behind Gordy and he turns to see Spud running toward the birds. "You birds you stop it," he shouts at the top of his voice. Punkass and Rags fly off in opposite directions.

"Gord ... Gord, you got guests. They're on their way coming up the stairs. I saw them."

"Who are they?"

"An old man and two kids."

The attic door creaks and Gordy and Spud turn to see Bernie leading Jessica and Cory out onto the roof.

"Bernie!" Gordy says as he clomps toward the old man and hugs him.

"Gordon, these are my grandchildren, Cory and Jessica. They wanted to meet you and your family. They call you the Pigeon Man."

"Hi," Gordy says. "Uh, this is my friend, Spud."

Spud holds out his hand. "Spud's my name ... Potato's the game."

Gordy explains. "Spud got his name from all the potatoes he eats."

"Who's the bird on your shoulder?" Cory asks.

"Oh, this is Trixie. She hatched some eggs the other day."

"Then how come she's not sitting on them?" Cory asks.

Spud explains. "Her old man, Big Daddy, takes turns with her."

Jessica hands Gordy a bag. "I brought some sunflower seeds for your family."

"Thank you," Gordy says as he crouches and takes the bag from Jessica, whose eyes widen on Trixie.

Jessica reaches for the bird, rubbing its breast, and Trixie coos at the child's touch.

Gordy stands and Trixie flies down from his shoulder to land on Jessica's head.

Cory is impressed at how relaxed his sister seems with the bird on her head. The boy gently nudges Bernie with his elbow. "Gordon, Cory would like to see inside the loft."

"Yeah, but you can't go inside," Spud says as Gordy leads the way to the loft.

Trixie flies off from Jessica's head, and the girl waves her mitten at the bird soaring above the rooftop. "Bye, Trixie."

Cory steps inside the loft while the others look in through the door. "Wow, this is a great bird home."

Spud stomps a foot down and shouts, "How come I wasn't allowed in the loft?" Nobody hears him and he runs into the building, bolting the door from the inside. "Now they can't get back in. They'll just have to stay on the roof. They'll stay out there until they beg me to let them back inside."

Gordy introduces members of his family to the visitors. "There's Big Daddy over there on the nest —"

"Who's that bird with the silvery feathers?" Cory asks.

"That's Rompin Ronnie. He's all shook up from a nasty encounter with some trouble-makers today."

A small bird flies down from a perch and lands on Cory's shoulder.

"That bird has a lot of pretty colours," Jessica says.

"That's Madonna. She hatched in the fall and Rompin Ronnie and the other … uh, playboys are already taking a fancy to her."

Madonna rubs her breast against Cory's cheek, and he laughs. "She tickles."

Spud unlocks the door and stomps back out onto the roof. "I was being selfish. Them kids just wants to see the birds. I can't lock nobody out from getting inside. That wouldn't be right."

OVERHEAD AND circling the roof, Rags glances down at a familiar form.

"Hey, what's that!" Spud shouts as something lands on his shoulder. Turning, he stares into two beady eyes. "Rags! You old orphan."

Spud has been warned about bringing Rags inside for a feed of potato peels in the kitchen. But he decides it's worth the risk. "C'mon, Rags. I cooked some fries this morning and I got some peels you'd die for."

TRIXIE GLIDES through the air, skimming soft breezes that cool her feathers with light snow. Here she is free again, with no eggs to hatch or Big Daddy to please. She sees some blue between the clouds and flies toward it. As if it were home.

Pruski's Walesa

PRUSKI HAS found a purpose for me. I am on my pillow on the bed waiting for him to rub my tummy when he leans forward with his big slobbery lips and kisses my face instead. I roll off the pillow onto my back, purring with eyes closed, and Pruski says, "I know what you want, Walesa."

I think he has received the message. At any moment his rough labourer's hand will press gently against my tummy and every nerve-end in me will tingle. Pruski's touch always transmits human brain waves – the kind that say, "I love you, Walesa, although you are Canadian cat." He actually says this to me.

It is true I am Canadian, but in another life I lived in Warsaw. We six cats from the same litter lived with a family named Czarnecki. The Czarneckis cared for us until the war started and they had to vacate the ghetto in a hurry. But the war was good for us cats. While food was scarce for humans, we feasted on rats and mice that were plentiful among the bombed and burnt-out buildings in Warsaw. The rodents were thin, but, as Pruski always says, "The meat is sweeter nearer to the bone."

Pruski's hand comes down and I feel his warmth drawing near. He takes my paw between his fingers, and I open my eyes to see him brush it through his whiskers. His beard is thick and furry, and when he takes me into his brawny arms and rubs his whiskered cheek against my head, it feels like the mother I never knew, but imagine knowing.

Perhaps it would be better if Pruski just trimmed his beard so he would not need to use my paw as a brush. I am probably the only cat in this miceless, ratless neighbourhood who serves a useful purpose. No cat of independent means would stand for it, but Pruski is a lonely man and he needs me.

He comes home to our basement flat every night and, before feeding himself, he opens a tin for me. If he is in a good mood, I am offered choices – as if it matters because he never listens to me anyway.

"Do you want tuna tonight, Walesa?" he asks, and I meow. "Or do you want *Liver Delite*?" Tuna is my favourite, but it doesn't matter if I meow for it, Pruski buys whatever is on sale – and this means I have an irregular diet. He will open a tin of *Liver Delite* and bend over my bowl with the spoon and say, "Do you want *Liver Delite*, Walesa?" I have tried putting my paw on the tin to restrain him, but he takes this to mean that I want whatever is inside. One time there was a tuna sale, and Pruski bought two cases. Despite this, every morning and evening he would ask, "Do you want tuna, Walesa?"

I am glad we do not have a TV. Most of the cats in our neighbourhood live in homes with noisy televisions. We have a quiet home in the basement where Pruski plays his records.

I remember the night he brought Wanda Landowska home in a bag with him. "This is a recording of the harpsichordist, Madame Wanda Landowska," he said. Since that night, Pruski and I listen to Wanda Landowska always after dinner. Landowska playing *Fantasia in C minor* is my favourite of hers, while he prefers Bach's *Concerto in D.*

Pruski sits naked on a chrome chair, the only chair we have, next to the bed where I recline and purr while the harpsichord's ubiquitous harmonies fill our modest room and he is lost in Landowska's *Goldberg Variations*.

But I am not jealous. Pruski's body has many broken and bruised parts, and I know inside him he is also hurt. When the music ends, I will jump down and rub his leg for all I'm worth and hope he will not push me away, or forget my name and call me "cat". He does not tell me where "Madame Landowska" takes him, and I don't wish to know. I have looked inside the human soul, and it frightens me. Pruski knows this from my eyes. My eyes tell him what I see, and that is why he never mistreats me. It is our understanding.

Last night, Pruski came home and said, "Tonight it is *Liver Delite*. You have no choice, Walesa. I had tragic day at work. You know what this mean?"

I lick my paw to clean my chin, then stare up at him. I know it means Ignace Jan Paderewski, and not Wanda Landowska. When he is in a dark mood and his courage needs bolstering, he invariably plays the great Polish pianist, composer and patriot.

I offer Pruski my paw. He brushes it through his beard, loosening some knots with my claws, and says, quoting Paderewski, "Let us brace our hearts to fresh endurance." He is always quoting Paderewski, whom I admire purely for his treatment of Chopin. Even in my past Polish life, I loved Chopin. Mr. Czarnecki would play the composer's nocturnes and preludes on the piano. "There is no greater composer of music for the piano than Chopin," Henryk Czarnecki would say. The whole family, including we six cats, would sit quietly and listen.

Tonight, Pruski boils cabbage for his dinner. Paderewski and cabbage. It is the formula for curing his dark mood. I hate the smell of cabbage, but if it cures Pruski, I'm all for it.

That night in bed, I snuggle next to him. He rubs my head and groans. "I had bad day today, Walesa. But I am thankful for you." Pruski cries into his pillow, and I know something is deeply wrong. "Today, I lose my job," he tells me. "I cannot afford food in can for you … Even when it's on sale."

Pruski had been out of work before. Once when he had been laid off, he told me: "If I don't work for one week, I know it; if I don't work for two weeks, my Walesa know it; if I don't work for three weeks, my landlord know it."

Pruski has always found a way to feed me. He will find a way. I am sure of this. I am sure. In Poland, at first I did not know how I would survive when the Czarnecki's fled. But we cats are resourceful. Pruski is also resourceful. Paderewski and cabbage will see him through.

A Life in the Day of Lonny Patrick

LONNY PATRICK rides the subway every day. When he can find a seat, he loses himself in the newspaper. His eyes get stuck inside columns of small print: obituaries, sports statistics, stock quotations, and classifieds. At each station stop, he glances up from a grey blur of type, but his eyes are vacant and only discern the movement of forms without faces or identifiable human characteristics – as if the world is inhabited by shadows. Lonny is comfortable inside the throng. This is how it is every day.

LONNY SITS on a stool at the coffee shop counter. There are reflections on the window, and he is one of them. A woman leans over his shoulder and orders two take-out coffees and a muffin. A voice next to Lonny asks if he will pass the sugar. He passes the sugar, but does not notice the hand that takes it has only four fingers. Lonny goes to the coffee shop washroom and stands in line until it is his turn at the urinal. After peeing, he washes his hands and wipes them with a paper towel that he crumples up and tosses into a wastebasket.

Someone has taken Lonny's stool at the counter, and pushes an empty coffee cup aside. Outside the coffee shop, a Chinese man plays a violin and some people drop coins into his basket. Lonny buys a bag of peanuts and *The Globe & Mail,* savouring the saltiness of the nuts he crunches in his mouth as he walks to the escalator. On his way down on the crowded escalator, for some unknown reason, patio stones pop into his mind. Lonny closes his eyes and sees white slabs of concrete. Someone's elbow jabs him in the ribs. Lonny jabs back.

On the train, Lonny leans against a pole and folds the newspaper. He reads all the figures on daily trading in Canadian mutual funds without once thinking of patio stones. He does not think of patio stones until the train pulls into his station, and he overhears a woman on the escalator talking about a patio party she had attended. He recalls his wife asking him earlier in the week to order the stones for the patio his brother-in-law promised to make for them. He had forgotten yesterday and the day before, and Marsha reminded him again this morning. His brother-in-law had phoned several times to ask if the stones had arrived, and each time Marsha had to make an excuse.

Lonny steps off the escalator and wonders if he will forget to order the patio stones today. He knows that if he remembers, Marsha will remind him about something else he has forgotten lately. Lonny thinks someone in the family is having a birthday party in the next few weeks. He thinks it might be Marsha's sister, Fern, but he isn't sure. Lonny sees people in queues waiting for buses. He asks himself, "Is it Fern's birthday?" as he lines up and waits for his bus.

On the bus, Lonny jostles for a seat. He sits next to a man with a turban and a beard. Lonny grew a beard on his holidays in the summer. Marsha hated it, but that isn't why he shaved it off. Lonny doesn't know why he shaved his beard off. He's not even sure what made him grow it in the first place.

Lonny gets off the bus and crosses the road with some school children. He walks up a street to the building where he works.

Inside the foyer, a voice says, "Hi, Lonny." Lonny doesn't stop to see who it is as he shouts "Hi" and runs to the elevator. He squeezes inside and smells a familiar perfume scent.

"Good morning, Lonny," the woman says.

Lonny turns and sees Bea. He smiles. "Good morning, Bea."

Lonny thinks Bea wants to have an affair with him, although no particular incident stands out. "I like your blue suit, Lonny," she says. "Is it new?"

"Yes, Bea, it is new. A new blue suit. I bought it last week. "

Bea and Lonny step off the elevator together. They walk to the same office and she holds the door open for him. "Thank you, Bea."

Inside the office, they stop next to a water fountain and Lonny asks if she would like a drink. "Thank you," she says and takes the paper cup from him, her hand brushing against his. They finish their water, crumple their cups and toss them into the wastebasket. One cup lands on the other, but Lonny sees no symbolic import in this.

Bea asks, "What's on your agenda today, Lonny."

He sighs. "I'm behind in my paper work ... and there's something about patio stones ... also someone's birthday...a party I think."

"How about lunch at that new place."

"Do you mean the Italian restaurant?"

"Antonino's, yes."

"What will you order, Bea?"

"The linguini."

"The linguini's good there, is it?"

"Succulent," Bea says, smacking her lips lasciviously.

"I really should pass on lunch and catch up on my work."

"I'm treating, Lonny."

"All right, Bea," Lonny says. "All right ... Antonino's it is."

Lonny goes to his desk and sits across from Bea at hers. Every few minutes he glances up and sees her smiling at him. His phone rings. It's Marsha calling to remind him about the patio stones.

"While I have you on the phone, Marsha, could you tell me whose birthday it is next week? Your mother! I thought it was Fern's. Oh, Fern's is next month. Okay."

"Somebody's birthday?" Bea asks as Lonny hangs up.

"Ah, it's nothing," Lonny says and goes back to his work. After a while, he looks up at Bea. "Bea, tell me something."

She comes over to his desk. "Yes."

"Do you think I'm dull?"

"No, not dull … . Just impenetrable. You strike me as someone who is all locked up inside. A man needing release."

"Release! From what?"

Bea shrugs. "I don't know. Perhaps any number of things; marriage, your job, your role model as a father –"

"Could it be patio stones?"

"I would never have thought about that."

"But you see, that's the problem. My wife has been asking me to order these patio stones for the past four days, and I keep forgetting. I have an excellent memory for details, Bea, but I keep forgetting simple things like patio stones and birthdays. I just don't understand it."

"I hope you don't forget we are having lunch today," Bea says as she walks back to her desk and Lonny admires her ample posterior.

At Antonino's, Bea points out the window at a building across the highway. "That's where I live."

Lonny finishes chewing his veal and turns to look. "You don't live far from work," he says. "You're close, Bea."

"I often go back to my apartment for a quick lunch."

"Quick, that's the operative word for our culture, isn't it?" Lonny says. "I hate how everything must be quick, you know. I don't like it. People need to take their time. I think it has something to do with the mess we're in … you know, socially and everything … like rush rush rush … everything must be done and disposed of … expedited or fast like food and sex to order."

Bea brushes Lonny's hand. "You're so deep."

"No, I just take time to think things through. But while I'm doing that, everything and everybody just rushes by."

"Would you like to have lunch at my apartment sometime?"

Lonny sips on his wine and smiles.

"Sure. How about tomorrow?"

ON HIS WAY home on the subway, Lonny remembers that he has forgotten to order the patio stones again.

A Father Missing

TIM KNOCKS *on the rooming house door. It opens slowly.* He sits on a park bench and imagines this: *Tim stares at the closed door and knocks again.*

He imagines various scenarios. A door opening and a door remaining closed: *A short thickset man with matted grey hair and a ketchup-stained undershirt answers – or a tall, balding man in a grey sweater opens the door.*

Tim wonders if either of these men is his father. He imagines the door again and knocks: *A tall scrawny balding man in a ketchup-stained grey sweater answers. Tim introduces himself. The man draws a blank on Tim's name – or hugs him, weeping and laughing all at once, "My son … My son … ."* Tim does not want to be hugged and gushed over by a father he has not seen since he was five years old. But neither does he want his long-lost father pretending he doesn't know him. Tim reminds himself it's been twenty-one years since his father left.

A pigeon swoops down and lands at Tim's feet to nibble the leftover crumbs from his ham and cheese on a kaiser bun. Tim wonders, "Did Mom ever send him a picture of me? Did he ever write to ask for one?"

When Tim was ten years old, he wrote to an address his aunt gave him. His mother was not supposed to know. He sent a photograph of himself and asked his father "Send me a picture so I will know what you look like." He is still waiting for a reply. *Tim puts his ear to the closed door and listens. Faintly, he hears a radio, or TV. It's either a football or basketball game. Maybe his father has fallen asleep watching TV – or he is listening to the radio with a beer in one hand and a cigarette in the other. Tim thinks he smells smoke, and he imagines his father's bed on fire. These things happen in skid-row rooming houses where people drink and smoke. The burnt mattress ends up smouldering on the lawn outside.*

TIM PICKS crumbs from his pants like lint and tosses them to the pigeon: *He knocks on the door and waits. He hears nothing. Maybe his father is asleep, or reading. He remembers Mom telling him that his father was quite a reader when they were married. Tim is also a reader. A woman answers the door. Tim introduces himself. "Hello, my name is Tim Connor. I'm Les Connor's son." The woman is about to speak when a man's voice roars behind her. "Who is it?" The woman turns. "He says he's Les Connor's son." The man roars again. "Tell him to go away." The woman's eyes narrow sympathetically on Tim. "Sorry, we don't know nobody by that name." She starts to close the door, but Tim stops it with his foot and shouts to the man, "Are you my father?" The man gets between the woman and the door. A face flashes before Tim as a thick, hairy arm draws her back into the room and the door is slammed in his face. Tim stands as if bolted to the floor. He hears the woman speaking, and the man roaring above her voice, "I ain't his goddamn father."*

Tim wonders why he imagines the worst about his father. Maybe it's this neighbourhood. As a child, none of his dreams about his father included skid-row missions and rooming houses, burnt mattresses and doors slammed in his face.

Last week, a friend of Tim's who volunteers at a local mission said he had met a man named Les Connor: "He's a tall guy with thick grey hair … and he walks with a limp," his friend said.

The next day Tim went to the mission and asked the regulars

about Les Connor. One said, "Les, he don't come here no more. Not since he met up with a woman."

Another said, "I was up to his room drinking beer with him last Monday night. I didn't see no woman, and he didn't say nothing to me about no woman."

Someone else said, "Les has a lady named Sandy he's livin' with, but he don't drink beer. Les just drink wine."

Tim even asked a neighbourhood cop who dropped by the mission regularly. "What did you say his name was?" the cop asked.

"Connor. Les Connor," Tim told him.

"Oh, Les … Les Connor. Sure, I know him. Les lives over at 137 Maxwell Street."

Tim remembers thinking, a cop would know these details and more about people. So he asked. "Is Les Connor tall with thick grey hair – and does he walk with a limp?"

The cop shrugged. "No, Les Connor is … I'd say Les was short and almost bald. And I don't recall a limp." The cop asked a group of men sitting around a table. "Does Les Connor have a limp?"

They all shook their heads, and one said, "Les is a sprightly little guy."

"Little!" Tim says.

"Les don't weigh no more than me … and I'm 140 pounds soaking wet," the man laughed, baring his gums.

Tim went to 137 Maxwell Street. The landlord answered the door and told him nobody by that name lived there. The cop must have been wrong about the address.

TIM BRUSHES the last crumb from his pants and walks over to the water fountain. He sees an old woman and a little boy take his place on the bench just as he puts his mouth to the gushing water and drinks. He starts walking. Tim thinks the cop gave him a wrong address. A landlord must know who lives in his house. But maybe the cop was right, and the landlord really didn't know anyone by that name. Transients come and go in these rooming houses. How can a landlord keep track of names? Slum landlords only keep track of rents and welfare cheque days.

TIM FINDS a stool at the Confederation Grill. He squeezes between a woman in sunglasses who is writing notes in a pad, and a mailman whose bag Tim rests a foot against. He orders coffee and watches himself stir it in the large mirror on the wall across from him. He didn't shave today. Who would notice around here? he thinks. The mailman gets up and a waitress says, "Don't you just love these welfare cheque days, Jim?" The mailman rolls his eyes and groans as he draws the bag onto his shoulder. "Yeah, one more street to do, then I can knock off for the day and cure this hangover at the Royal Oak."

Tim's friend had told him about welfare cheque days. "It's quiet in the mission on cheque day. They're all out drinking wine or getting stoned on cheap drugs."

Tim asks the mailman, "Did you deliver to Maxwell Street today?"

"Oh yeah, Maxwell and Perth and Shelbourne and –"

"Did you deliver a cheque for a man named Les Connor on Maxwell Street?"

The mailman cocks his head and looks at Tim as if he is crazy. "You think I remember names?"

On his way out the door, Tim imagines a cheque for his father in the mailbox on the wall of 137 Maxwell Street.

TIM SEES four men on the porch as he opens the gate and walks up to the steps. Two of the men are standing. One is holding a bottle of wine. The other two sit on an old, tattered chesterfield. "Excuse me, I'm looking for a man named Les Connor."

The men look at each other.

"Don't worry, I'm not a bill collector."

The men seem amused by this, and Tim realizes they are not the kind of people who worry about paying bills. But he knows he must allay any suspicions they might have.

"And I'm not serving a warrant."

The men heave a collective sigh and relax, and Tim knows he has struck a chord.

One of the sitting men asks, "What you want Les Connor for?"

"He's my father. My name is Timothy Connor."

A man stands up from the chesterfield. He is precarious and can barely keep his balance. The man is short, balding, and wears a clean undershirt with his ribs showing through. His eyes are watery and red-rimmed. The other three men leave.

"I'm Les Connor," the man says.

Tim leaps up the stairs and hugs Les. He holds him and doesn't want to let go. The lost years mean nothing now. No recriminations. He has lived and died for this moment, and he won't let it slip away.

Les is like a skeleton in his son's arms. Tim holds him up. "I never stopped hoping I'd find you."

Les pats him on the shoulder, "All right … . All right … ."

Tim relaxes his hold, and Les looks up into his face. "You've grown some since I last saw you, Tim. You were playing with toy trucks on the floor the day I left. That's the way I wanted to remember you."

Tim asks, "Did you ever think about me?"

Les shakes his head, "Not often … sometimes."

Tim looks around. "This is a slum, Dad. I don't like to see you living like this. You deserve better. Look, you're just skin and bones. You can't be happy here."

"Down here everybody's accepted for what they are … not who they are, or what they own," Les tells him. "Nobody expects anything else from a person."

Tim recognizes himself in his father's words. Tim had always thought, people can either accept me for what I am or screw off. I won't be made over in their image of me. He had often wondered if his father took off because he could never be the person Mom expected him to be. Tim didn't want to make the same mistake. "Dad, I'm hungry. How about you? Let's go over to the

Confederation Grill for supper. It's on me."

Les frowns. "Save your money, Tim. I've got a tin of tuna upstairs. We can toast some bread and make sandwiches."

Tim follows his father inside the house. "Do you have any mustard pickles?"

Les stops on the step and turns. "How'd you know I like mustard pickles?"

"Mom told me when I was a little kid how you liked mustard pickles. So I got to like them too."

"Damn, I spit you right out of my mouth."

Mrs. Wilmont

DIANE SQUINTS through the windshield, her headlights on the sign up ahead. Rain slashes in diagonals across the smoked glass, and her windshield wipers work to clear the dark onslaught. As she sweeps past the sign on the post, Diane reads: ADAM'S JUNCTION.

She repeats the directions Joseph gave her earlier that day ... "Five miles north of Adam's Junction." Diane switches on the radio and static scratches the air around her. She changes stations, her hand frantic on the buttons – but each blasts static from the speakers. Electrical charges crackle around her. Even her favourite station, the one with 24-hour news, whose signal exceeds all others in sheer kilowatts, rings with static and warped voices. She tilts her head toward the speaker on her left, eyes fixing on the road and broken lines that bend through the streams washing over the windshield. The voices waver and music crosses the frequency: a piano concerto, its sound resonant and clear.

Diane turns the radio off. If she cannot tune in the 24-hour news station, she will listen to no radio at all. She hates classical music. Diane hates anything classical, although once a man told her that she had a classical nose. She suspected the flattery was intended to arouse a less classical part of her anatomy. Her nose was not impressed.

Rain batters the roof overhead. Diane sees another sign on the road, this one bent from the storm. "It must be Pyke's Road, the turn-off," she tells herself. Diane stops and squints through her window at the crooked sign. She can make out the Y and the K. But that is all she can read before lightning explodes in her rear view mirror, and she steps on the gas.

Diane stretches her arm across the seat and taps her fingers on the brown-paper package. She is tempted to hold it up to her ear and shake it. Something inside had rattled when Joseph handed it to her earlier that day.

Joseph had been good to her. He let her use his apartment while he was in Australia. He lent her money to pay off her bank loan. Joseph was her saviour. Now he asked for a favour in return. "Deliver the package to a man named Wilmont," he told her. "He has the only house on Pyke's Road."

Diane doesn't know if Wilmont is the man's first or last name. She has never known anyone with a name like that before. Wilmont, she thinks.

"You don't even have to get out of the car," Joseph told her. "Once you stop in front of his house, just sound the horn and he'll hear you. He'll come out and take the package from you. It's that simple."

"That must be the house," Diane mutters as she turns down a gravel road. The rain has slowed.

She sees a light in a room on the bottom floor of a two-storey farmhouse. Diane pulls up next to a late model half-ton truck and stops. The sky is quiet. She lights a cigarette and stretches her legs. Drawing a deep breath, she sounds the horn – a long, bleating siren tone. Diane pats her forehead with a handkerchief, and waits. She sits upright in her seat when she sees the front door opening. A short man limps down from the porch. "Is he ... Is he wearing anything?" Diane asks herself.

The silence after the rainfall and the sombre, misted countryside has become unbearable. Diane turns on the radio. The piano concerto again. Brahms, or somebody. She turns to the news. Diane turns up the volume: "The Israeli-occupied West Bank and Gaza Strip are sealed off by the army –"

Rolling down her window, Diane calls to the man. "Are you Wilmont?"

The man does not answer as he limps toward her. Diane switches on her headlights. He is naked, and short enough to be a midget. Joseph did not mention that Wilmont was a midget, and had a bald head.

As he limps closer, Diane becomes more repulsed by him. Large rolls of fat hang in layers from his chest to his hips. A tiny, shrivelled, uncircumcised penis jiggles as he walks. Diane want to turn her face away, but decides to keep her eyes on him.

"Are you Wilmont? I have a package for you – from Joseph."

The man limps out of the glare of the headlights. "Where the hell did he go?" Diane shouts as the door on her right slams shut.

She bolts around and faces the man sitting next to her. Diane gasps. She has never seen a head that oblong before. He has no eyebrows, and his eyes are like large, grey indistinct puddles. His mouth is a small slit above globular jowls, and he has no chin. The man reaches for the package.

"Get out of this car … Get out," Diane shouts as she pulls off her spiked shoe.

She hears a groan and, although his mouth has not opened, she knows it came from him.

"Take your goddamn package and get out," Diane screams again as she raises her shoe.

He tears open the package, his small pointed fingers clawing at the paper and throwing it back over his shoulder.

"Joseph said you'd take the package and leave. Now leave … or, goddamn, I'll bash you with this shoe."

The man holds the box up to his face and tears it open with his teeth, spitting bits of cardboard all over.

"Get out," Diane shrieks as she slams her shoe against his bare skull.

The man does not flinch at the thud, or when blood oozes from his wound and streaks his face. He just looks into the box and smiles.

Diane pushes her foot against him. "Take your package and leave."

"Oh-h-h-h," the man growls at the back of his throat as his eyes roll to their whites.

"What is it?" Diane asks.

The man lifts an object from the box and shows it to her. "My wife."

"Wilmont ... if that's your name ... Wilmont, I want you to take whatever you have there and –"

Diane stops. Wilmont holds the object to his cheek and makes a purring sound. His eyes are half-closed as he rocks his head from side to side. For a moment, Diane feels ashamed at having struck him. But he does not seem bothered by her assault, or the blood streaming down his face.

"My wife ... Mrs. Wilmont."

"What? Who?"

The man unfolds the object and holds it to his mouth.

Diane switches on the interior lights to see what he is up to.

Wilmont's chest heaves as he blows into the object that swells with each lusty puff. Red painted toes pop out, then ankles, calves, rounded knees, and legs netted in factory printed stockings.

Wilmont stops blowing, but continues to pant. He gazes down at the rounded thighs in his arms and his lips tighten around the words: "My wife ... Mrs. Wilmont."

Diane is nauseated from the smell of perspiration, that sickly odour mixing with blood.

Wilmont resumes his blowing and puffing on the object until a full-blown inflatable woman with a red wig beams seductively into his face – and he kisses her lovingly.

"All right ... That's enough," Diane says. "Take Mrs. Wilmont back to your house and live happily ever after."

"Thank you," Wilmont whimpers as he opens the door.

After he climbs out, Diane slams the door behind him, locking it and starting the car. Wilmont crosses the headlights with the bride cradled in his arms. Diane curses Joseph. Why hadn't he warned her about Wilmont?

Diane's car edges down the gravel road and stops. Glancing back, she sees a light flicker on through the curtains of a second floor window. Diane thinks she hears a piano concerto and wonders where the music is coming from. She rolls down her window and looks back at the house. Behind the second floor curtains, two silhouettes dance.

Ragtown

"WHEN THEY bulldozed Ragtown and built those apartments back in the fifties, they wiped out our culture overnight," Scotty says from the back seat as the car turns south of the housing project. He looks out at the red brick high-rises towering above the cracked pavement and garbage-strewn sidewalks. "They tore up our roots and ripped out our hearts in the name of slum clearance. Because it wasn't middle-class culture, it couldn't be legitimate as far as the social engineers were concerned. It's how the institutions have been treating Indians and blacks in this country for over a century. And we were white. So it must be class discrimination."

Denise glances over her shoulder at the old man in the back-seat. "You're at your irascible best today, Gramps."

"Was Ragtown as bad as those projects?" Ken asks.

"No, we lived in houses. Our homes were ramshackle because the slum landlords never fixed them up. But most people kept them clean. We had streets with trees and gardens. In the summertime, the backyards were overrun with gladiolas and sunflowers. Where are the streets in that ghetto? Or the gardens?

It's goddamn concrete and asphalt. It's infested with cockroaches and rodents, and the so-called socialist and liberal councillors in this city are being driven around in limousines and voting themselves pay raises. We are choking on moral hypocrisy. The people in that ghetto are piled one on top of the other. That's no good for families with children. It's soul-destroying. And soon it will be society-destroying."

Denise turns to Scotty, "Gramps, how are your hands today?"

Scotty holds them up. "After all the bones I broke in these hands and couldn't even hold a fork, I'm not worried about a little arthritis."

"I brought a camera so we can snap some pictures of Cork Street," Ken says.

Scotty sighs. "Yes, it's all that's left of the old neighborhood."

"Gramps has a photo of Cork Street the way it was in 1935."

"1936," Scotty says as he holds the photo up and sees himself sitting on the front step while his sister, Kate, and two friends play double dutch with skipping ropes on the sidewalk.

A WOMAN'S hoarse voice shouts from a second-floor window, "Scott! Scott, you get in here."

The girls stop skipping and Kate says, "Mom sounds mad."

Scotty climbs the rickety steps to the second-floor kitchen and recognizes Mrs. Kearney's shrill voice talking above his mother's. He knows why she is here and stops at the door of the kitchen.

Scotty's mother grabs him by the shirt and pulls him inside. "Mrs. Kearney says you beat up her boy."

"Mike called me a carrot-top again, Mom. He's always calling me names."

"You are a carrot-top, boy. You better learn to live with people calling you names coz you're a queer-looking duck."

"I can't help how I look."

"But you can help hitting people," Mrs. Kearney says. "You're just too free with those fists."

"Do you know Stewart Kearney?" his mother asks.

"Yeah, he's Mike's big brother."

"Well, he's itching to lay a beating on you for what you done to Mike. Mrs. Kearney wants you to promise never to hit Mike again, or she won't be able to stop Stewart from getting revenge."

"Tell Mike not to call me names," Scotty yells at Mrs. Kearney.

His mother cuffs him across the face. "Don't you talk to your elders with that tone of voice. I raised you better than that."

"How did they ever miss Cork Street when they tore down the old neighbourhood for the projects?" Ken asks.

Scotty looks up from the photo. "It was a little backstreet tucked in among old factories and warehouses, south of the main residential core. So it had to do with zoning."

Denise looks at the posh condominiums and town houses lining the streets two blocks south of the ghetto. "Cork Street must be like a time warp, looking back to a simpler time."

"Everything is simple in hindsight," Scotty says as he sees the corner where once stood a popular neighbourhood beer parlour.

SCOTTY RUNS for the door of the Derby Tavern with Stew Kearney close on his heels. The roar of the men crowded and drinking inside the beer parlour explodes in his ears as he dashes past tables and lunges for the back door.

"There's gonna be a fight," a waiter yells.

"Who?" someone asks.

"I don't know. Two kids."

Scotty stumbles over a pile of bricks in the back lot and falls. He looks up at Stew standing over him. Stew smiles and kicks him in the face. Scotty rolls over in pain, blood spewing from his nose.

"Let the kid get up. C'mon, fight him fair," a man hollers.

Scotty climbs to his feet.

Stew lunges for him and Scotty lands a solid left hook to the jaw. Stew reels, dropping to one knee.

"Put the boots to him, kid," someone yells.

"I don't need to," Scotty hollers as he waits for Stew to get up. Scotty ducks under a flailing right hand and lands a three-shot combination that rattles off the face. Stew's knees buckle and he staggers back against the wall. Scotty closes in, both fists battering the face to a bloody pulp.

"It must've been unbearable living down here. All those old factories spewing chemical pollutants from dawn to dusk," Ken says.

"I remember waking up to the stench of the big smokestacks and roar of machines every morning. We heated our house with coke we picked out of the hot ashes once the gas company had extracted what it wanted from the coal then dumped the rest. They just let us take it."

SCOTTY PUSHES the rusty wheelbarrow through the large open gate. Kate follows, carrying a shovel. The grey sky drizzles across the yard where Ace Fuels had dumped the remains of coal processed in its plant, leaving chunks of coke smouldering in ash piles. Shadowy figures, scattered across the yard, work among the fuming mounds. The stench of coal tar and oil hovers over the yard.

Scotty looks up at the clouds thickening in the November sky. "We better work fast, Kate. It's gonna start raining hard any moment now."

Kate digs into the mounds with her shovel and drops neat piles on the ground for her brother to sort through. Scotty crouches, his hands lifting solid chunks and tossing them into the wheelbarrow. Some pieces are hotter than others and burn his hands. He works quicker as the heat intensifies.

"Don't burn your hands," Kate says.

"I'm all right," Scotty says, wanting to appear brave for his sister.

The six-o'clock whistle blasts across the coal yard. Soon, the dreary streets fill with armies of soot-faced workers – and convoys of crowded streetcars seem to emerge from nowhere, clanging along old steel tracks.

Scotty straightens up and wipes his forehead just as Mrs. Mullen crosses his field of vision. Her son pulls a wagon behind him, followed by two other children. Mr. Mullen died in the summer when he fell from a steel beam on a construction job. As an occasional worker, he had no pension or other benefits, and he left his wife penniless with three small children and another on the way.

Mrs. Mullen crouches, her large stomach bulging behind an old threadbare coat as she searches for coke among the ashes. She glances up when Scotty approaches. "Mrs. Mullen, let me do that for you."

"Oh, you're the Dugan boy," she says.

Scotty is surprised at how drawn and pale the woman has become since he last saw her at the funeral. Her blue eyes appear glazed over and almost lifeless.

Mrs. Mullen draws herself up as Scotty goes to work, tossing chunks of coke into the tin wagon.

"Father Walsh brought me a small sack of coal last week," she tells Scotty. "But he has a lot of needy parishioners, and I can't expect his help all the time."

"This coke burns longer than coal," Scotty says. "It'll see you through to next week. I'll come by with more then."

"Did you ever work in any of those dirty old factories, Gramps?" Denise asks.

"You see that building over there with the boutique and the café with people sitting outside? That used to be a mattress factory. I worked there for four years before turning pro. I came out of grade school and right into the factory. High school was out of the question for me and most of the kids in the neighborhood. Even if we wanted to go to high school, our parents couldn't afford the clothes or the books."

"Now you can't move in your house for books," Denise says.

"Until I started working at the mattress factory, I had only read comic books and pulp westerns. That's where I met Parker. He was the boss's son, and something of an intellectual. Actually, anyone with an idea about anything was an intellectual to me back then. We became friends, and Parker introduced me to Voltaire and Marx, and to Steinbeck's and Hemingway's novels. I don't read comic books anymore, but I still enjoy a good western."

"Denise showed me your press clippings from when you were a professional boxer," Ken says. "You won your first fifteen pro fights."

"Fourteen by knockout, and one by TKO."

Denise laughs. "How come you couldn't knock him out?"

"That was Toots Morgan. Tough as nails and a good street fighter, but he had no style in the ring. He couldn't keep up with my footwork. I wore him out by the third round and started using him as a punching bag. But the stubborn oaf wouldn't go down. No matter how hard or often I hit him, I couldn't close the deal. I couldn't send Toots to the canvas."

SCOTTY'S FACE is soaked with blood, some of it his own from shots he had taken in the first two rounds. He squints to see Toots on the ropes. The crowd is howling for a knockout as Scotty presses the attack and lands successive blows with both fists, knocking his opponent's mouthpiece out. Toots clings to him, and Scotty looks into his face. Both eyes are swollen and closed, and Toots says, "You better kill me. I won't go down." Blood squirts from Toots's face as Scotty opens a gash in the corner of the left eye. The referee shouts for him to stop and he retreats.

Scotty dances around the ring with arms raised in an uproar of boos and cheers; boos from those in the crowd who felt cheated out of a knockout and cheers from the others who enjoyed a good fight.

KEN TURNS down the narrow street and parks. "Well, here we are. This is Cork Street."

Denise helps her grandfather out of the car and Scotty steps onto the sidewalk, balancing himself with his cane. "Looks like they fixed up the old houses."

"There are no poor people living here any more," Ken says.

"We weren't poor," Scotty snaps. "Poor is a state of mind we couldn't afford. We were working class."

SITTING IN his new Plymouth convertible with Bess Walker, Scotty hears the jingle of an ice cream wagon and sees the kids dashing past.

"I remember when I couldn't scrounge a nickel for a cone," Scotty says.

Bess runs her hand through his hair. "And now you're a rich boxer."

"I'm gonna buy the kids all the cones they want."

"Don't forget me, I'm a kid too," Bess says.

"Strawberry ... right?"

Scotty walks up to the wagon and flashes a wad of bills. "Hey, give me a strawberry cone. Then give these kids anything they want. I'm paying."

"Our family lived at 10 Cork – that house across the street. And your grandmother lived two doors down at 14."

Ken snaps pictures of both houses.

"Gran once told me you won her heart through strawberries."

Scotty laughs. "Bess was crazy for strawberries. Strawberry ice cream. Strawberry jam. Strawberry tarts. Or just fresh with a little sugar. I always said Bess had strawberry cheeks."

"That's right," Denise says. "Gran had the loveliest red cheeks right up until her illness."

Scotty crosses the street and stands before 14 Cork. Denise follows him. "It was a sweltering July night ... two days into a heatwave that lasted a week. Bess and her friend Geraldine were sitting right there on the front steps. I had been away for almost a year with bouts throughout the Maritimes and down into Maine and

Massachusetts. I promised your grandmother I'd write, but I never did. So I owed her an apology. "

"Excuse me, Geraldine, do you mind if I have a few words with Bess?"

Geraldine stands to leave, but Bess tugs on her friend's skirt. "No, stay. I don't talk to liars."

"I want to apologize," Scotty says.

"I don't accept apologies from liars."

Scotty sees that Bess is not wearing the engagement ring he gave her the year before.

"I better go," Geraldine says as she stands and leaves.

"Why didn't you write like you said you would? You wrote to your mom. She told me."

Scotty crouches next to her. "I was ashamed to write to you."

"Ashamed of what?"

"Bess, I was with other women."

Bess hauls off and smacks Scotty, knocking him back on the sidewalk. "You bastard! You disgusting no good bastard. I waited for you because I thought we were engaged. I turned down some good men. I hate you. Get out of my sight, you scum!"

Scotty rubs his jaw. "I think this is a technical knock out."

"Get away from my door! You're not welcome here no more."

Scotty climbs to his feet and brushes himself off. "I'm sorry I let you down, Bess," he says as he turns and leaves.

"Get back here!" Bess shouts. "I'm not finished with you."

Scotty walks back and Bess hands him the engagement ring. "Here give this to one of your whores."

"That's in my past. It's behind me."

Bess cries. "I never been with no other man but you."

Scotty gets down on his knees. "As God is my witness, I promise I will be faithful to you."

"Get off your knees, you fool. People will wonder what's going on."

Scotty takes her hand and puts the ring on her finger.

"What happened to your hand?" Bess asks.

"They took the cast off last month. It was broke so bad the doctors told me I can't fight professionally no more."

"I'm a fool to forgive you, Scotty. I deserve better than a washed-up prize fighter with no prospects."

"I know that, Bess."

They sit on the steps and kiss harder and harder, their bodies entwining.

"Bess, it's cool down at the lake. What you say we go for a swim and make up for lost time?"

"Do you have protection?"

"No, but I thought if I propose an August wedding and you say yes, maybe we can make a baby tonight."

"Where did you learn that?" Scotty asks as he lies back on the sand.

"What?"

"You know, being on top of the man."

"I overheard my aunt telling Mom how it drove her boyfriend wild."

"Wild isn't the word for it, the way you were grinding your hips into me. It felt like the head of my dick was spinning off."

"Not bad for a beginner, huh?"

Scotty draws her down on the blanket and kisses her belly. His tongue continues exploring until his face moves between her legs ...

"So Gran must've forgiven you or I wouldn't be here."

Scotty smiles. "We made your mother that night."

"And you had the wedding reception at 14 Cork."

"It started at 14 Cork, but every house on the street partied right into the next day. We went into every house for toasts, and there was beer and wine and food in all of them."

"Just one big celebration."

"Well, not exactly. One of the wedding guests decided he wanted to challenge a pro boxer. You get used to that sort of thing and try to laugh it off because your fists are dangerous weapons. But when he came at me with a broken wine bottle, I popped him. It was so easy, I felt sorry for the guy. When he woke up the next morning, I put a cold beer in his hand. Then there were two or three fistfights out on the street that night. But we all came together the next day to lick our wounds. We packed all the kids from the street into the back of the pick-ups and went for a picnic out at the Rouge Valley."

"Gee, you guys lived colourful lives."

"We didn't see it that way then. But when I look at how artificial life has become with governments and corporations running people's lives, I'm reminded of Orwell's prophecy. It's worse than when the Church ruled because then you could always hide in sin."

"I got some great photos," Ken said.

Denise looks at her watch. "We'd better go. The reception starts at three."

AT THE HALL, a large man with a bald head greets them and shakes Scotty's hand profusely. "I'm Baldy Connors."

"Baldy! The best goddamned fighter to come out of the neighbourhood."

"Yeah, street fighter, maybe, but I never had your class on the canvas, Scotty," Baldy says, his voice like a steel shovel being dragged over gravel.

"Yeah, I had class all right," Scotty laughs. "I was a ballerina in the ring."

Baldy leads them to their tables. "Sure, Scotty, you was a dancer, but that left hook of yours was savage."

Lloyd Cully steps up to the microphone and the roar in the hall subsides. "Ladies and gentlemen, I welcome you to our neigh-bourhood reunion. The idea for a reunion came from Freddy Lester and his wife Jean. Most of you old timers recall that Freddy and Jean owned Lester's Delicatessen. They kept the neighbourhood in pastrami and debt for many years. The Lesters worked for a year contacting people all over the country at their own expense. For this we owe them our gratitude and thanks."

People stand to applaud the Lesters.

"Our neighbourhood produced many fine Canadians forged by the work ethic, belief in family and love for our country. We served honourably in two world wars. We produced actors of stage and screen, writers, professional athletes and a governor general. And we are very fortunate to have as our master of ceremonies a man who has published many novels and stories. He was born in a modest house on Oak Street, one of ten children. I am pleased to introduce Jack Holt."

A slight man in an over-sized grey suit limps onto stage to a standing ovation. He stands at the microphone with head bowed as people whistle and cheer.

"Thank you, friends. You will be happy to know that I climbed back on the wagon to be here. That's how important this occasion is for me. The only other time I'm sober is when I'm working on a novel. I never touch the booze when I'm writing. I came here tonight to be with my old friends and reclaim my working class roots. Although writing novels brought me some fame, it did not make me rich. I managed to ascend to the giddy heights of the lower middle class. I also came here to make a confession. I want to confess that some of you here tonight were the inspiration for several characters in my books. One character especially comes to mind. If you will bear with me, I will read a brief passage from a book called *Ragtown:*

> When the feisty little flyweight, Danny Brooks, returned to the neighbourhood from the battles of the ring, he was a target for every punk seeking a reputation. This included the cops who badgered him at every turn. Danny knew if he laid a hand on one of the bulls, it would mean a trip to Cherry Beach late at night. Danny's hands couldn't punish in the ring anymore, but with a few deft left hooks to the head he could knock any amateur on his ass. When Patty Grogen, who ran the local gym, organized a card of fights

between the cops and local pugilists, Danny was asked to compete in a five-rounder. The proceeds would go to a camp for neighbourhood kids. Danny agreed, but said he wouldn't need five rounds.

On the night of the fight, Danny climbed into the ring and met his opponent, a tall cruiserweight cop. Next to the cop, Danny looked like a pale, freckled kid who hadn't eaten for two weeks. His ribs were like a cage – his heart like a hawk beating its wings inside.

The bell rang and Danny went into his dance while the big cop closed in to maul him. Danny felt the cop's fists fanning the air around him while he jabbed and moved, jabbed and moved. His jabs didn't seem to bother the cop who shook them off like mosquitoes stinging his face. Danny knew he wasn't in condition. He hadn't trained since his last fight two years ago. He dazzled the crowd with his footwork, but realized he had lost some of his speed and maneuverability. His counter punches were off target and grazing his opponent's head, but not landing with any force. The cop kept coming at Danny until he caught him between the eyes. Danny's knees buckled and he dropped in a heap. The bell rang and he picked himself up from the canvas and staggered to his stool in the corner.

'Stop with the footwork … You're attacking from too far outside,' his corner man said as he wiped the blood from Danny's face. 'Go at him. Use your hand speed. You have to get in close … Get in close … Use your hand speed, Danny.'

In the second round, the cop came out ready to finish Danny, whose left eye was swollen. Danny knew his mistake was trying to put on a show for his fans. He could do that in his prime, but this was a finale. Danny was over the hill and knew he would never step into the ring again. But he could not allow a cop to beat him, or he'd never hold his head up again in the neighbourhood. The cop pressed the attack and Danny clung. The referee drew them apart. The cop moved in again, expecting Danny to dodge and weave. Danny surprised him by planting his feet where he stood. The cop could not believe his good fortune as he swung for Danny's head. The punch went south and Danny responded with a quick right cross that knocked the cop's head back and gave him the opening he needed. He went to work in close, jabbing, jabbing, and jabbing until his left arm tired. His right fist ripped the nose open, and blossoms of blood spewed into the smoky air. The cop careened backwards into the ropes. Danny showed no mercy, pouring on the leather until the referee stopped the fight."

"Jack Holt wrote that about you, Gramps," Denise says.

Scotty smiles as Baldy leads him toward the stage.

"That passage was inspired by one of Canada's greatest boxers, Scotty Dugan. He's here with us tonight. And he's ready to rumble. Please give it up for Scotty Dugan."

Baldy leads Scotty onto the stage and up to the microphone while the hall shakes from applause and cheers.

Bent over and leaning on his cane, Scotty is also shaken by the tribute. "I ... I really don't know what to say. Thank you for remembering an old pugilist and inviting me here tonight. I thought I was a footnote in a forgotten history. I'm an old man now with many grandchildren, but I still remember the neighbourhood. The values we learned there are sadly ignored in our society today. I hope you will be patient with an old man who has something to get off his chest. Maybe I'm a dinosaur whose time has passed. But on our way to the hall today, we drove by a ghetto that was once our neighbourhood. And only a few blocks away, we saw luxurious condominiums and town houses. So the gap between the wealthy and the poor is being stretched to the breaking point. But, surprise, we are seeing acts of barbarism in quiet middle class neighbourhoods. Children shooting children.

Parents killing children and children killing parents. Dead babies being tossed into dumpsters. Or murdered before they are born. What does all of this mean? I earned my livelihood in a brutal profession. Some people called it barbarism. But those people never had to fight their way out of a slum. Jack Holt did it with a pen. I did it with my fists. Nobody ever did it by crying poor or sitting on their ass waiting for a handout. I don't know if there is a god, although at my age I should check that one out just in case. But I know there's a human spirit, and we humans are not just organisms and machines. Our spirituality is all we really have. There is a poverty in society worse than any slum; the poverty of the spirit. Well, I just want to say people have to fight for their spirituality because society won't do it for them.

"I have one more thing to say. I wasn't the best boxer to come out of the neighbourhood. That distinction goes to the late Frenchy Bélanger. Frenchy could break every bone in your face in a street fight or in the ring and go to St. Paul's on Sunday and pray for you. He was French and a Catholic in an Anglo-Protestant neighbourhood, so he had to be tough. Frenchy never invested his earnings as my Scottish mother and Irish Dad insisted I do. He lived in the fast lane with fast women and faster cars. He ended up back in the neighbourhood broke and working as a waiter and bouncer in beer parlours. I stopped by to see Frenchy a few times, and I couldn't believe how... how he kept up his spirit."

Scotty gulps for air. "That's all I have to say."

Jack Holt returns to the microphone as Scotty is led off the stage to applause. "Scotty, for years I felt guilty about including you as a character in my novel. I felt I owed you a percentage of my royalties. So I'm relieved to know that I needed the money more than you."

Scotty stops amid the laughter in the hall and says something.

Jack Holt shouts, "What did you say, Scotty?"

The laughter subsides and Scotty repeats himself, "I said you can discuss royalties with my attorney over here."

"You brought your lawyer with you?"

"Yes, this is my granddaughter, Denise."

Denise stands to acknowledge the applause.

"Denise," Jack Holt says, "your grandfather appeared on fifteen pages in my novel. How much do I owe him?"

Denise huddles with Scotty, and says, "I guess we can settle this out of court if you come by for dinner one night with a bottle of imported malt scotch and a signed first edition of *Ragtown*."

Ghetto Boy

PERCY FALLS back on the lawn, his feet on the sidewalk, and looks up between tall buildings at the sky. His eyes follow a big silver jet flying at supersonic speed through the blue. Percy wonders if it's the plane taking his friend Ambar to India with his grandmother. Ambar left this morning, and already he misses his best friend who will be gone for a month.

Percy had waited a whole year to turn fourteen, and he and Ambar had celebrated his birthday by going to a Raptors basketball game. The Raptors won, and everything about being fourteen promised excitement. Then along came the summer holidays and Ambar's news that he was leaving for India. Percy wonders how he will fill a whole month of summer without his best friend.

Percy hears someone shout, "Hey!" He looks up as JoJo's bicycle skids to a stop, the front wheel nudging Percy's untied running shoe. "Hey, Percy, I could've run over your feet, man. Why you lying there with your feet on the sidewalk anyway?"

"I don't know. I just feel like it."

"Well, you better be careful nobody run over them and break your toes," JoJo says as he pedals away.

Percy sees the jet disappearing into the clouds. Maybe it's not the plane with Ambar on it. Maybe it's flying south to Jamaica. Percy would love to go to Jamaica just to see the Streamertail Hummingbird. The librarian told him there are only twenty-four of these birds on the island, and they can't be found anywhere else in the world. Percy took the book with a picture of the Streamertail Hummingbird home and tried to draw and colour it in his notebook. He showed the picture to his teacher who said he had an artistic bent.

"Percival, boy, you just turn fourteen, don't you know how to tie your shoe laces yet?"

Percy looks up at Mrs. Bunting's large round face smiling down at him. "Yeah, I do."

Mrs. Bunting crouches and starts to tie one of his shoes and Percy pulls his foot away. "No, I like them that way."

Mrs. Bunting groans as she straightens up and shakes her head. "I'm glad I'm not your mama, that's all I can say."

"Me too," Percy says under his breath as he wiggles his toes in his shoes and sighs in relief. Mrs. Bunting walks on, her big booty shaking like vats of Jell-O.

The sky is empty but for some clouds that take the shape of things in Percy's mind. He thinks one cloud looks like a Streamertail Hummingbird until it turns into a dragon's head. Percy thinks dragons are real and live in cavernous mountains in Northern China, these Dragon Kings only revealing themselves to magicians who travel from all over the world to visit them and their temples. He read that, or heard it from someone. He's not sure which.

"Percy!" a voice shouts angrily at him. "Get off that lawn! Don't you know junkies leave their dirty needles in the grass."

Percy looks up at his older cousin, Rodney, and shrugs. "There's no needles here."

"I guess if there was, you'd have one in your ass by now."

Rodney walks on and Percy thinks if he feared all the terrible things that happen in the project, he'd be nervous all the time.

His mama says don't go near the playground where a kid was stabbed to death last week. But he goes, and it doesn't bother him. His uncle says don't go to the store for that pimp and crack dealer, Carter, who gives him a dollar just to go for smokes. Carter doesn't bother him, and Carter's girlfriends gush over how cute Percy is. They invite him into their apartment and he goes inside sometimes because they keep lots of candy for that sweet tooth they have when they're stoned, which is all the time. Once, at Carter's apartment, he sat on the sofa between two ladies who smelled so fresh and good he forgot about the candy.

The ladies started tickling him until Percy was on the floor laughing his head off. One dropped little chocolate rosebuds down his mouth and the other licked his tummy and made him really hard. Percy got scared when Carter came in and saw him on the floor being spoiled to distraction by his girlfriends. Carter had this look that could kill, and he pulled a knife from his pocket that snapped open with a blade long enough to cut clear through Percy's chest to the other side. The ladies recoiled and Percy jumped up, buttoning his shirt. "You can't afford these ladies, Percy," Carter said before breaking into laughter. Carter put his hand around Percy's shoulder and led him to the kitchen and a box of icy steaming popsicles of various flavours. "I think you better have a cherry popsicle," Carter laughed as he reached into the freezer. Percy grinned nervously and took the popsicle. "Now you run along, Percy, we're expecting some company."

PERCY SEES a girl on the fifth floor balcony, and he thinks it is the new girl in his class who moved into the building two weeks ago and always smiles cute at him. He thinks her name is Tamara or something that sounds like that. He can't think of another name that sounds like Tamara, so that must be it. He overheard her telling the teacher that her family just moved into the project for the time being until they get back on their feet. But everybody in the project says that.

And what's wrong with living here anyway? You can get shot or stabbed anywhere from what Percy hears on TV. You can get robbed in the better neighbourhoods too. He knows some older guys who do it – break and enter, burglary in neighbourhoods where rich folk spend more money on security systems than people he knows make in a year. He wonders why there's rich and poor. There'd be less crime if the rich would just share more of what they have. But they won't share. They want to keep it all to themselves, so it's taken from them by those who desperately need it. That won't be Percy because he's seen too many kids busted for stealing from the rich, and their moms breaking their hearts over the cops taking their kids away to prisons.

Percy wouldn't do anything wrong to hurt his mama because she'd kill him where he stood. Other mothers are not as tough on their kids, or they're out working and not around to kick ass – and the daddies are nowhere to be found. When he was five years old, Percy's daddy hit his mama, and she broke a bottle over his head. The police came, and the last he saw of his daddy was him bleeding out the door for the hospital to have his head stitched.

Ernest moved in last year. Ernest is a small man, shorter and a way thinner than Mama, but he works long hours driving taxi and brings home his money to the table. Percy doesn't call him Daddy, but Ernest is a good friend to him, and he loves his Mama, so he's cool. Once Ernest got tickets for a Blue Jays game, and he took Percy and Ambar and they saw Carlos Delgado hit a home run to the upper deck. Ernest was just like a kid jumping up and down. Percy was a little embarrassed, and later reminded Ambar that Ernie was only his stepdad.

Percy sits up. The girl on the balcony is waving at him. He waves back just as Todd runs up from behind and puts a hold on his neck. Percy and Todd tumble back in the grass and wrestle, squirming in and out of head locks. Todd pins him and Percy looks up at the girl who has stopped waving. "Okay, you win, Todd. Now let go."

Todd lets go and jumps up. "I saw you waving at Tamarind. She's my girl, you know."

"I didn't know that."

"She was waving at me when I came out on my balcony. Then I saw you waving back."

"I didn't know. I thought she was waving at me."

"Why would she wave at a skinny little prick like you?"

"Because she's sweet for me and I got the killer charm ladies love," Percy says as he starts running.

Todd chases after him into the building and down the basement steps. A woman carrying a laundry hamper up the steps blocks Todd and shouts, "Why you chasing that boy who smaller than you?"

Todd shrugged.

"You so big and look at him. He just a baby."

"But we're the same age," Todd explains. "We're both fourteen."

"You just get your ass out of here," the woman shouts at Todd who takes off.

The woman pats the forlorn Percy on the head. "Are you all right, boy?"

Percy looks up at her. "Uh huh, I'm just out of breath from running."

POLICE CRUISERS surround the building and Percy sees cops with bulletproof vests going inside. Percy hears shots fired. Later an ambulance arrives and he pushes through the angry crowd to see Carter on a stretcher. People are cursing the police, and Percy overhears someone say it's just a shoulder wound. "You be cool, man," Percy shouts as Carter is being placed in the ambulance. One of the ladies Percy met at Carter's apartment and another, a blonde he has never seen before, are led out of the building in handcuffs. They are frisked by women cops and put into the cruiser. Percy hears a familiar voice behind him and turns to see Tamarind.

"Hello, Percy."

Percy feels his throat go dry and his face flush. He stammers, "Hello, Tamarind," barely able to mouth the words.

"I saw you wrestling with Todd. I hope he didn't hurt you. He's such a bully."

Percy catches himself shaking his head, and then nods, "Yeah, he hurt my shoulder. But once my Mama rubs it with liniment, I'll be okay."

Tamarind smiles. "My brother plays basketball and he has me rub him down with alcohol. He says I have soothing hands. Would you like me to rub your shoulder?"

"Sure, but where?"

"Up in my apartment. My mama's working late and my brother's out of town at a basketball tournament."

On the elevator up, Percy is at a loss for words. Tamarind feels his discomfort and says, "I hope you don't think I'm a bad girl for inviting you up when my Mama's not home."

"Oh, no," Percy says. "It's nice you do that … ask me up for rubbing my shoulder."

Inside the apartment, Tamarind helps Percy off with his shirt and he lies back on the sofa. "Which shoulder hurts?"

"Both hurt. Todd really pounced on me."

Tamarind starts working the cooling alcohol into his skin, and Percy thinks he will faint. He feels his temperature and the rest of him rising. His heart races as Tamarind's hands seem to mould his emotions. She leans forward and kisses his lips, and he gives himself over to her.

"Is this your first time?" she says, opening his pants.

Percy gulps, "Yes," as he looks into Tamarind's face smiling down at him. He blushes and turns away until she leans forward, giving off a scent that intoxicates and maddens him. Percy feels crushed under her hot breath, her tongue on his neck. He finds himself making strange growling sounds he had never made before or even imagined having inside him. Percy closes his eyes and a Streamertail Hummingbird appears, its iridescent green in flight through a red-streaked sky. He opens them on Tamarind, and she is more beautiful than anything he can imagine.

Jim's Shirt

J IM'S PLAID shirt hangs in an empty closet as if it is waiting for him to wear it again, as if he can. It has been alone on the hanger since Terese put it there last week. She keeps track of this and other memories from her brief life with Jim.

She remembers the Sunday afternoon when they met at an outdoor jazz festival, the first time they made love on a rainy autumn morning in a small room with a big squeaky bed, the day she introduced him to her parents at a family picnic and her mother dropped a bowl of potato salad at his feet, the night they parked on a cliff overlooking a lake where moonlight shimmered on dark waters and the sky brimmed over with stars – and Jim proposed, the Saturday morning in April at 11:37 a.m. when he slipped the ring onto her finger and kissed her while family and friends looked on in the hushed church ... and the evening last week when she learned Jim would never come home again, that his body was in a morgue somewhere, broken and twisted from the highway crash where they had to cut parts of him loose from the metal.

Terese wanted to know who would cut her loose from Jim's death, who could come close enough to put her back together again.

After the funeral, Terese had her sister arrange for all of Jim's clothes to be given to the Salvation Army, but she kept the green plaid madras shirt she had bought him on their first wedding anniversary. He wore it to dinner at LaScala that night, and every time Terese touched it, she felt as if she was touching him.

"Do you really like the shirt, Jim?"

Jim took Terese's hand in his and brushed it against his shoulder. "It feels so good I feel like I'm wearing you, Terese."

"Really. Do you mean that?"

"I've never said anything I mean more."

"The salesman told me it was lightweight and cool."

Jim sipped at his wine and felt Terese's leg under the table. "Just like you."

Terese smiled as she fanned herself with her hand. "I'm lightweight and hot. I think the wine's gone to my head."

"I'm feeling it too, Terese."

"I like the button-down-collar look on you, Jim."

Jim filled their glasses to the brim "You certainly know how to button down a guy."

Terese thought about what Jim had said. "Have I done that to you?"

"Before I met you, Terese, I was walking around with empty button holes. And you filled them all."

"I buttoned you down."

"For good."

"For good! Is that good, buttoning someone down? Isn't that like tying someone down?"

"Uh huh. Except they're buttons, not rope – and I was more than willing."

"So, Jim … do you like the … uh, that patch pocket on your shirt?"

"I'd like it more if you were biting through it."

"I can arrange that," Terese said as she pulled her chair up next to his and started nibbling through the fabric.

"Terese, I think we better finish our wine and leave. It's getting too hot in here."

Terese opened the buttons at the front of his shirt. "I want to play."

"So do I. But not here. So cool it."

Terese ran her tongue down his chest to his navel.

"Terese, did you know the cuffs on this shirt have a two-button adjustment?"

The couple at the table across from them stared reproachfully. "C'mon, Terese, people are looking at us," Jim said as he waved his hand with the glass in it at the couple, and splashed some wine on the floor. "Terese, do you want me to blow my buttons here?"

Terese came up for air, bit his neck and whispered, "No, later I'll blow them for you."

A WEEK HAS passed since Jim's coffin was lowered into the ground. Before going to bed, Terese opens the closet door and stares at his shirt. Over and over, she remembers the morning she last saw Jim walking out the door, saying, "I'll call you if I have to work late tonight, Terese." Terese looks at the shirt hanging alone in the closet and shouts, "Jim, I'm too fucking young to be a widow. Why did you have to die on me? It's not fair when all I ever did was love you."

Terese wears Jim's shirt to bed with her that night and falls asleep. She has a dream where Jim comes into the room and lies down next to her. He holds her close to him and says, "Don't wake, Terese. If you wake, I'll be gone and never come back again."

"I don't want to wake without you, darling," Terese tells him as she snuggles in, and the empty pill bottle falls from her hand to the floor.

Sid's "Bosch Stone"

WHEN SID told Hatty over breakfast he had decided to get a tattoo, she didn't believe him. Since they were kids, Sid enjoyed getting a rise out of his sister. Like that bitter cold winter when he told her he was going for a swim in the lake. Hatty didn't believe him even when he came downstairs in that ridiculous bathing suit he called his "slingshot"

"Don't forget to take a towel," Hatty had said as Sid stepped outside into a mound of snow on the porch.

After Mom died five years ago and she and Sid inherited her house near Kew Beach, Hatty was the only woman who cared for him. She knew he took her caring for granted as he had with their mother. Two wives gave up on him. One son from the first marriage never visited or called on the telephone, even after Sid's kidney operation – while a daughter from the second marriage called only at Christmas time. Sid had retired last year after working for twenty-five years as a clerk at the post office. Fifteen years ago Shirley left him, and took Joey. He had visitation rights, but Shirley put so many obstacles in the way of him seeing his son that he finally gave up – although he continued to make his monthly payments. Shirley had convinced Joey that Sid had deserted him. The next marriage came apart after eight years when Sid finally mustered the courage to confront Joan about her affair with the accountant next door who visited on the pretext of doing her books for the quilting business she ran out of the house.

If Sid was bitter about his marriages, he kept it to himself. Hatty felt it would be good for him to open up to her – the one person he trusted. But he never raised the subject, and he seemed to have left his past behind. So she kept quiet. Her own life had been over and under the rocks a few times, and perhaps it was fitting that a brother and sister who rarely saw each other in their early adult years should come together after the death of their mother to reclaim their affection, and what remained of family.

Hatty had expected Sid to burst through the door, shivering in his swimsuit. But when ten minutes passed, she put on her coat and boots and stepped outside, then back inside to get Sid's coat from the closet.

"Where did that damn fool go?" she asked herself repeatedly as she made her way down to the beach with the coat on her arm. Hatty gasped when she saw two figures in swimsuits in the distance, on the beach, running into the water. "Sid! Are you crazy?" she shouted. "Sid, you'll die of pneumonia! "

Hatty knew she was too old for running in the snow like she and Sid had done when they were kids in Haliburton and had vast fields to romp in. They weren't kids anymore. Hatty stepped down from the boardwalk just as the two figures emerged from the water. "Sid, I brought your coat."

Two young men in bathing suits walked past her. "I'm sorry. I thought you were my brother."

When Hatty returned to the house, Sid was reclining on the sofa, sipping on a hot cocoa and reading the newspaper. She could barely resist the urge to suffocate him with his own coat.

"Where have you been, Hatty?" he had asked.

"I thought you might need a coat."

"Oh, I changed my mind about going for a swim. I came in

the back door and went down into the den."

Hatty had sighed and put Sid's coat back in the closet.

AT BREAKFAST, Hatty fixed tea for her and Sid.

"It's the big day," Sid said as he patted his ass.

Hatty stirred her tea. "What day?"

"The day I get tattooed. Right on my ass."

Hatty sat next to Sid at the table and sipped from the cup. "What! A tattoo. Why are you ... Did you say on your ass?"

"That's right, Hats. Right on the ol' keester."

Hatty rolled her eyes to the ceiling. She once knew a man who had a big pink rose with a dagger through it tattooed on his chest. Roses have never smelled the same for her since the weekend she spent with those petals that seemed to peel off in her heated mouth. But Sid was nothing like that cowboy in studded leather. "So why are you tattooing your ass?"

"Maybe I'm sick of other people doing it for me. This time, I'm in control."

Hatty's hand started shaking, and she set the cup down in the saucer, spilling some tea. She glanced up at Sid and her eyes said, *Why are you trying to shock me all the time?*

"You know, Hats, you'd look good with a tattoo."

"Where, on my keester?"

"Yeah, well, why not? Or ... on one of your breasts. You know, some men go wild for women with tattoos."

"Ah, men," Hatty said, almost spitting the words out. "I don't trust any of them."

"Does that include me?"

"I love you, so I guess I have no choice."

"Are you sure?"

"Well, love isn't something you make up your mind about, Sid. It's what a person feels. Don't you feel that way about me?"

"No. I honestly don't, Hats. I can't love anymore. I gave love all the chances one person can in a lifetime, but, as fortune or misfortune would have it, we just never clicked. No, I can't say I love anybody."

Hatty knew she couldn't criticize Sid for his failures in life when her own past was a disaster. She often wondered how she had become a varnished replica of her mother. Hatty regretted that she had pitied her mother. You're not supposed to pity someone who you love. That's a coward's excuse for love.

"So what kind of tattoo are you getting, Sid?"

"I want to surprise you."

"I'm too old to appreciate surprises, Sid. So just tell me. Is it a flower? Or an eagle?"

"Na, all those traditional tattoos are boring."

"Please, Sid, promise me one thing," Hatty said as she walked Sid to the door. "Promise me it won't be Elvis."

Sid laughed. "Why Elvis?"

"Why? Well, because you tell all those jokes about Elvis being alive. And because you're aware that I visited Graceland and slept outside the gates when he was really alive. Because you always joked about the time I threw my panties on the stage at the Elvis concert in Toronto. You would do something like that just to shock. You're spiteful that way."

"Elvis on my keester? Gee, Hats, you must think my life revolves around annoying you. I really don't plan it that way."

HATTY WORRIED all day about sterilization. Dirty tattoo needles leading to hepatitis, AIDS or other diseases. Surely Sid would have enough sense to find a reputable … what are they called … tattooists?

"I am a Body Art Technician," the man on the telephone said.

"My brother is presently considering having a tattoo … uh, put on him. And I'd like to know if tattoo shops are approved by the Board of Health … you know, regulated?"

"We are a Body Art Studio. Anyone who creates body art, whether by tattooing or body piercing, is highly regulated."

"So all your needles are clean."

"Once we use a needle, we *dispose* of it. All tattoo tubes and grips are ultrasonically cleansed. And our studio is cleaned before and after – "

"With disinfectants? What about gloves?"

"Of course, we wear disposable gloves."

"So you throw them away afterwards."

"Yes, that's what disposable means."

"I know, but I just thought I'd ask."

"Why don't you and your brother visit our studio, and we can discuss these matters further."

"That's a good idea. But could you tell me what's *in* for tattoos these days. You know, when I think of tattoos, I think of eagles and mermaids, or, you know, some people like Elvis ... so you can see how out of date I am."

"Not necessarily. Celtic symbolism is the rage now, but many people like traditional designs. Yesterday, I did a fire-breathing dragon on a lady's ... uh, shall we say groin area? We've done five anchors on arms this week. Anchors on arms and, let's see ... and roses on breasts and tummies are still popular."

"No kidding ... roses. Have you ever seen a rose with a dagger through it?"

"My uncle had one."

"Your uncle!"

"Yes, but he had it surgically removed."

"What a shame. Why did he do that?"

"My aunt made him do it for her own reasons."

"I once knew a man with a tattoo just like that. It had a rose with a dagger through it. But there were tears dripping from the pink rose petals."

"Only one of those was ever created by the inimitable Bosch Stone."

"Who?"

"Bosch Stone. He is to tattooing what Salvador Dali is to painting. He's a genius. Stone never makes the same tattoo twice. He *will* do traditional tattoos, but they all have his distinctive style. Or as Bosch Stone would say ... 'I make an indelible statement'."

HATTY REMEMBERED the tears dripping from the pink rose petals … how hot and steaming they were when she kissed them. For the rest of her life, she will remember the wild growling man she tamed to a purring pussycat. He wasn't the only cowboy in her life, but that's another story.

Hatty heard the key turn in the door and she went to the kitchen.

"Hats," Sid shouted from the hallway.

"I'm in the kitchen, Sid."

"Hats, I want you to meet Irma."

"Who?" Hatty asked as she turned to see Sid standing next to a woman with a mass of frizzy grey hair spilling out from under a tartan tam.

Irma's voice was raspy. "Pleased to meet you, Hatty. Sid told me all about you."

Irma held out her hand, and Hatty recoiled when she noticed rings on every finger and a tattoo of a swan on the woman's forearm.

Sid turned away and went to the fridge. He took out two bottles of beer. "You want a glass, Irma?"

"Na," Irma said as she uncapped the bottle and took a swig.

Hatty poured a glass of warm water from the sink, and her hand shook. "So, Sid, did you get your tattoo?"

Irma laughed and Sid joined in with his familiar cackle.

"What's so funny. Were you just joking about getting one?" she asked with her back to the couple.

The laughter became more boisterous.

Hatty turned to see Sid and Irma with their arms around each other.

"Sid mentioned you were nervous about him getting a tattoo," Irma said.

Hatty bristled inside even as she smiled politely. She wondered if the woman, whose name she had already forgotten, could sense her hostility.

"Hats, you have the honour of seeing two indelible Bosch Stone creations."

"Bosch Stone!"

Irma swallowed the rest of her beer, belched, giggled and stood next to Sid. They both turned, drew down their trousers and underpants, and bent with full asses bared to Hatty, who gasped. Two halves of a heart that, when joined cheek to cheek, read: *Sid and Irma, lovers always.*

Hatty wanted to throw up. Her whole body shook and, momentarily, she thought she would faint. She grabbed onto the sink and shuddered.

Sid and Irma started laughing again and Hatty shouted, "Pull up your pants and get out of this house. Both of you … Get out!"

"I planned to leave anyway, Hats," Sid said.

"You're not my brother, Sid. You're not anything to me."

"I'm packing my suitcase and getting the fuck out of here," he hollered as he left Hatty alone in the kitchen with Irma.

"I'm sorry you're upset about Sid and me," Irma said,

"You don't love Sid. You're like all the other women who used him and left him with nothing to hold onto."

Irma took another beer from the fridge, uncapped it and took a long swallow. "You think I'd have Sid's name tattooed to my ass if I didn't think we were permanent … if I thought there'd ever be another man?"

"You don't love my brother."

"How do you know that? What makes you so goddamned high and mighty to know who loves who? Sid has a right to his own life. You've given up on yours. So let him live his."

"Sid doesn't love anyone."

"Oh yeah, well I have a tattoo on my ass to say he's been there. And that's what really pisses you off, ain't it?"

"C'mon, Irma," Sid said as he stood at the kitchen door with his suitcase.

LATER THAT night, Hatty lit a candle and carried it upstairs to the room with a view of the lake. She stood at the bay window with the flame held near her face and looked past her reflection to the trail of moon on the waters. The house was quiet without a man in it. She blew out the candle and wondered how long Sid would be away from her this time.

TONY HAILS a cab and climbs into the back seat. "Take me to the bus terminal."

The driver sneers at him in the mirror. "The bus terminal's only ten blocks away. You can walk there."

"What are you talking about? It's at least fifteen blocks from here."

"I said you can walk to the bus terminal. Now get your ass out of my car and start walking," the driver shouts.

"Hey, buddy, I'm staying right here, and you're gonna drive me to the bus terminal. I have rights, you know."

The driver turns and says, "Tony, get your ass out of my car before I kick it out."

Tony's face brightens. "Eddy, you old fucker. You're still driving hack."

Eddy moves out into the traffic. "Yeah! What about you? What are you doing?"

"Ah, I manage this singer named Johnny Silver. He's coming in from Kenora on the bus."

"Is he good?"

"Unbelievable! The kid can sing country, rock, blues and jazz, and he writes his own songs. I'm negotiating a recording contract for him."

"You ever hear from El?"

"No, not since that day at the Heron Lake Cabins."

"Shit, that was fifteen years ago."

"Those were great times on the road with El, Eddy."

"But we blew too much money on booze and dope."

"I don't regret that. We were living on the edge and digging every minute of it."

"That concert El gave at Guido's Roadhouse was incredible. I have it on video and it still gives me chills."

"Was it really fifteen years ago?"

"Yeah, back in 1985."

Go Cat Go

S TAGE LIGHTS dim on El's face in a blue sweat. His voice in tears and saxophone ... . *"Only fools rush in."* Backstage, Eddy pans the audience with his video camera. "He has them fainting, Tony."

Tony draws on a joint and passes it to Eddy "I never saw El so fucking cool ... Not since –"

"Yeah, Sudbury. "

"I was gonna say Timmins, but ... yeah, Sudbury he brought the house down."

Eddy inhales and hands it back.

Tony squeezes the joint between tweezers and puckers for a drag. "I always said El's only as good as his audience ... and that night they was rocking in Sudbury."

"Yeah, he brought the house down with *Ready Teddy.*"

At the footlights, El's down on one knee. He catches a pair of panties from a woman in the front row and wipes pearls of sweat from his forehead. "Thank you, little honey ... *coz I can't help falling in love with you ... .*"

The stage to black. El bows in a spotlight, spreads his royal cape to the crazed roar surging, sucking him into the undertow. For a moment, lost in applause, he imagines that the redhead in the front row is Rhonda.

Lights up. El blows a kiss as he bounds off stage.

Eddy's waiting with a towel. "Shit, El, they're banging their seats for more."

El snatches the bottle of Southern Comfort from Tony's hand and takes a long gulp. "Looks like I got me an encore. Hey, Eddy, grab my guitar."

"Give 'em *Hound Dog*, El," Tony yells.

El hangs the guitar around his neck and combs his hair. "Remember this morning in the van ... what Arf done to my snakeskin boots."

"He shit on them," Eddy laughs.

El grabs Eddy by the throat. "Listen up, boy. My hound don't shit. He messes. Know the difference?"

Tony gets between them. "All right ... Ease up, El. Eddy's just joking."

El mocks a scowl. "He's always making dogitory remarks about Arf."

Tony laughs and shakes Eddy. "Hey, Eddy, El was joking too. You were both joking."

Eddy rubs his neck and smiles. "Yeah, we were being funny."

El bounds onto the stage and shouts at the house band. "Hey, boys, don't you mess on my snakeskin boots."

El opens his black sequinned shirt to reveal the tattoo on his chest ... a large pink rose with a dagger through it and blue tears dripping from its petals. The beat begins and women in the front row are restrained from climbing onto the stage by security guards.

"*Well, it's one for the money ... two for the show ... three to get ready ... now go cat go ... but don't you mess on my snakeskin boots ... you can do anythang you wanna do, but, hey, little honey, don't you mess on my snakeskin boots ... boots boots snakeskin boots ... you can do anythang you wanna do, baby, but don't you mess on my rattlesnake boots.*"

EDDY BACKS the van up to the rear exit. Pink and blue neon lights from Guido's Roadhouse flash in the rear view mirror.

El staggers out with Tony. Arf barks behind them. El climbs into the back with his hound while Tony sits up front next to Eddy. They take the highway north.

"We get cash?" Eddy asks.

"Na, the fucker gave us a goddamn cheque after he promised cash," Tony complains.

"Guido wants me back in November, Eddy," El says as he collapses on the mattress and uncaps a bottle of Southern Comfort. Arf snuggles next to him.

"How much?"

"Five hundred," Tony says as he lights up a joint.

"That's it? El packed the place. We should have … "

"I know. I was expecting at least eight hundred cash. Everybody's paying in cheques on this tour."

"Hey, pass that joint back here," El shouts. "Let's get real gone."

"Why don't you crash, El? You need the sleep," Tony says.

"How can I sleep with Rhonda on my mind?"

Eddy laughs. "El, you haven't seen Rhonda for thirty years. You get more love from groupies than you ever did with her."

"Leave him alone," Tony mumbles.

El draws on the joint and hands it back to Tony. "Eddy, remember what Bosch Stone used to say?"

"Oh, you mean the guy who tattooed your chest?"

"What Bosch Stone done on my chest is art. He's a genius, man."

Tony laughs. "He reminded me of some old-time beatnik with that beret and the goatee."

"Remember the night he was playing the bongos, what he kept chanting over and over?" El asks.

Tony snaps his finger. "Yeah, he kept saying, 'This is Blissville.'"

"Yeah, Blissville. That's how I feel now. Like I'm in Blissville,"

El says as he rolls onto his side with his back to Arf, pulls his cape over his face and slides into a pit of sleep.

Tony glances back. "El's sleeping."

"That's good," Eddy says. "He really put out tonight."

Tony laughs.

"What's so funny?"

"Guido told El he was the best goddamn Presley impersonator he ever had at the Roadhouse."

"Oh, no!"

"Well, Guido meant it as a compliment ... but you know El."

"What did El say?"

"I felt sorry for him. He just went limp and told Guido, 'I ain't personating nobody.' That stunned Guido, who looked at me real funny as if, you know, El was crazy."

El crawls forward and puts his hands around Tony's neck. "Who said I was crazy?"

Tony removes his hands. "I thought you crashed."

El yawns. "I think I wanna sleep in a real bed tonight. Eddy, stop at the next motel."

"Shit, El," Tony says, "we got over six-thousand in cheques, but only $42 cash. Nobody's gonna cash a cheque from cats who look like us."

"What's wrong how we look?"

"You kidding?"

Eddy laughs. "I'd say he was kidding."

"So Eddy's got a bad case of pimples and a leg disability," El says.

Eddy nods. "I'm the only forty-seven-year-old guy in Canada with teenage acne."

El musses Tony's hair. "And Tony's got them little pink-rimmed slits for eyes. He looks like Elmer Fudd."

"Nobody's gonna cash a cheque for us," Tony insists.

El rubs his chin. "Well, maybe we can find somewhere real cheap."

AFTER TWENTY miles of lonely road, Eddy's headlights flash on a sign: HERON LAKE CABINS.

"Hey, I got an idea," Eddy says. "It's late September. I bet there's some vacancies. Maybe we can get a cabin cheap."

The van pulls up next to a row of cabins by a lake. "You guys wait here," Tony says as he climbs out.

El and Eddy get out to stretch and sniff the fresh country night air while Tony pushes the buzzer by the office door.

A man opens the door a crack.

"I see you got vacancies," Tony says.

The man nods. "We have some cabins available. How many of you are there?"

"Just me and my two buddies and a hound dog. We been on the highway most of the night and we're really bushed."

The man opens the door and Tony steps inside.

"We usually charge $85 a cabin, but it's off-season ... So how's $50?"

Tony winces. "Gee, that's $15 more than we got in cash, and I guess you don't take cheques, eh."

"No, I'm sorry."

A woman in a housecoat with rollers in her hair steps out of a back room. "What's seems to be the problem?"

"This man and his friends want to rent a cabin, but they only have $35."

"That's okay," she says, and takes a key off the wall."

"Gee, thanks. We really appreciate that."

The woman nods and hands Tony a card. He fills it out and hands it back.

"Tony Castillo! I knew a guy by that name," the woman says. "I was good friends with his sister, Lucy."

"I got a sister named Lucy. Hey, what's your name?"

"Rhonda Webb."

Tony slaps his forehead. "Rhonda! You're the Rhonda Webb who used to date my buddy El?"

"Oh, Elmo ... What a character he was. He begged me to

marry him. Whatever happened to him?"

Tony shakes his head. "You don't wanna know."

"He's all right, isn't he?"

Tony nods. "Oh, yeah, he's all right. He's … well, a lot like how you knew him back in the 50's."

Rhonda rests her elbows on the desk and looks wistfully at Tony. "I was fifteen then, and Elmo was sixteen. I fell in love with his duck's tail. I always thought he looked like Elvis. How is he?"

"Why don't you ask him yourself?"

"You mean he's here? You guys are still knocking around together after all these years?"

"Yeah, El's a performer now, and I'm his manager. We just did a gig … uh, a concert, but we got paid by cheque. So we're strapped for cash."

"Gee," Rhonda says, "I don't want Elmo to see me looking like this with curlers in my hair. What if you guys come over for breakfast in the morning. It's on me. I'd like to surprise Elmo. I have a sixteen-year-old daughter who's a dead-ringer for me when I was her age. There was a 50's dance at her school in the spring, and she can wear the get-up I made for her then."

"Hey, you don't know how thrilled El will be," Tony says. "Maybe 'shocked' is a better word."

TONY SHAKES El and wakes him. "It's seven-thirty a.m., El."

El opens a bloodshot eye, sees Tony and pulls the blanket over his face.

Tony shakes him more vigorously. "C'mon, El, you know you need a half hour to comb your hair – and them nice people is expecting us over for breakfast at 8."

El climbs out of bed and stretches. "I certainly don't wanna disappoint them nice bacon and eggs … I mean people."

Eddy comes out of the washroom with a razor to his soapy face. "Don't be so sure it's bacon and eggs, El. Remember that bed and breakfast place we stayed at in Sarnia … They served muffins and granola."

"Hey, I didn't eat none of that middle-class crap."

Eddy points at El. "That's right. You practically knocked over the breakfast table and stormed out the door."

"Yeah, I found a little place down the street with a breakfast special, where I could drink coffee and smoke and listen to Dolly Parton on the jukebox."

El steps outside the cabin with Arf behind him and sniffs the scent of bacon. "Hey, boys, I think we're in for a real Canadian breakfast."

Eddy looks up at the dark, drizzling sky. "Shit, I just put on my shoes and it's already an ugly day."

El follows behind Tony and Eddy with his cape blowing around him.

They find a table in the middle of the small dining room. "You do the ordering, Eddy," El says as he pats Arf's head. "I don't talk to no strangers before noon."

From the kitchen, Rhonda and her daughter, Tara, hear the boys come in. They peek out. "They're weird-looking guys, Mom," Tara says.

Rhonda puts her hand to her mouth and gasps. "Omigod, he hasn't changed."

"Mom, one of them men looks just like Elvis."

"Why didn't Tony tell me that Elmo was an Elvis impersonator?"

"Here comes the waitress now," Tony whispers.

"Good morning," Tara says with pencil poised to take their order.

El glances at Tara and leaps up from his chair. Covering his face with his hands, he stumbles to the door.

"You all right, El?" Tony shouts.

El rests his head against the wall. "I'm just feeling a little woozy. I think I'll go outside for some air."

El reaches for the door and feels a hand on his. He turns to see Rhonda.

"Hello, Elmo. It's been a long time."

"Rhonda?"

She nods. "Is that all you have to say?"

El hugs her. "Oh, honey, I've lived and died for this moment. Your face was never off my mind."

Rhonda kisses El's neck and he feels faint.

El eases himself out of the embrace. "But, Rhonda, you're a married woman. I saw your husband in the office."

"He isn't my husband. You remember Pete ... my brother."

"You mean you ain't married?"

"I was, but I kicked him out five years ago for cheating on me."

"I don't believe it," Eddy says as he climbs into the van. "El's giving up his career to settle down with his childhood sweetheart."

"There goes our meal ticket," Tony mutters. "Now I gotta cancel all the shows."

"I'm not worried," Eddy says. "I'll just go back to driving hack."

El and Rhonda walk over to the van with Arf yelping behind. "If you boys are ever by this way, stop in for breakfast," El says. They wave at the van as it moves down the gravel road and turns onto the highway.

"I hate stories with happy endings," Eddy says.

Name Withheld

VINCE IS his name. He has had this name for thirty-three years, and it is time to end it.

Vince jumps from his fifteenth floor balcony. He does this with arms spread.

It is how he planned it during lunch over quiche and a carrot muffin.

Vince falls. Into space. Through space. Both.

Either he is committing suicide or making a terrible mistake.

Vince will not read about himself in the paper tomorrow. Some things he will miss. The morning paper. Quiche. An occasional carrot muffin. Walks in the park.

Soon his head will mix with the concrete spinning below, redden all the cracks in the sidewalk.

Vince is wearing blue- and green-striped pyjamas in space. These are his favourite pair.

Directly in front of him is another high-rise. He is falling between it and his own. Both blur before him in a confusion of windows, balconies, faces.

There are people at windows. Even in the uproar of falling sky and traffic below, he hears them. The brave cheer him on. Others laugh. This does not make Vince feel wanted. If he were to cry, "SAVE ME," would they hear him? Would it matter?

Who are these people? Are they into bloodsports? or is it psychological kill? All brain matter, and no head.

They have cameras and are snapping and videotaping him. Only they hear the clicking and whirring, and see him – arms spread, frozen, or slow motion in space.

Vince's death will appear on the six o'clock news. Does he want this?

A thirty-three-year-old man, name withheld, jumped to his death while hundreds cheered him on.

A twenty-second slot on the six o'clock news. A blur between two high-rises. Wide angle. Vince, a speck. Or zoom lens on the face. You can make out the eyes.

Cut to the police. Ambulance. Crowds. Traffic. TV cameras. A witness says: "I saw him climb over his balcony. At the time, I thought it was funny. You know, a man in pyjamas. We all laughed and thought it was a joke, until he jumped."

Vince does not want his death televised. He does not like television. He has never owned a TV. He much prefers reading. Biographies are his favourites. Followed by fiction. Some poetry. And, of course, the morning paper. Vince hates what television does to people's minds. He believes television controls the central nervous system of the public. He refuses to let it control his. The thought of his death following commercials for super fries and the Pepsi challenge does not enthral him.

The man in the blue and green striped pyjamas is Vince. Nobody else made the decision for him to jump. He decided to die in those pyjamas. Now nobody can take his place inside them. It had not always been this way ... Vince deciding for Vince.

Others in other pyjamas decided for him instead. Always others.

Never Vince. Until now.

Until Vince thought of the six o'clock news. Thirty seconds. Hundreds of thousands viewing his death.

NO, Vince screams. He has decided against dying. He has decided. He has. He. Vince. Him.

Body Wire

09:37

PAT FEELS the fist at his throat, gripping the collar of his blue silk shirt. Shoved up against the wall, his head bangs on brick. He gulps to get his breath back. A square-jawed face of Neanderthal origin smiles up at him and snarls, "You wanna fuck with me?"

Pat gasps and the fist tightens at his throat.

"Know what I do to people who fuck with me? I introduce them to Junior."

Pat's eyes narrow on the cannon at the tip of his nose.

"This is playtime for me, Patty boy. I can waste you here in the alley. No sweat. Right up your fuckin' nose like the bluebirds of paradise … out through your head."

"No, Romy, don't."

Romy tightens his grip on Pat's collar.

"No, is it?"

"Let go … my throat, Romy."

"Ok, I'm letting go, but Junior stays."

In a cold sweat, Pat feels the breath heaving back into his lungs.

"I gave the ice to your bag bride ... just like Barnes told me."

"Which one?"

"Lucinda."

"Lucinda?" Romy's sinister smile turns to a scowl as Pat explains.

"Yeah, I met Lucinda at the Melody Bar. She looked lit up like white Christmas, and ready for another sleigh ride. Only I didn't think it should be in the snow I am told to deliver ... because Lucinda is sitting with some dumb-looking John in the bar. I figured his eyes were sharper than how he talked, or the way he dressed like a used car salesman out on the town for a hooker. Maybe I'm paranoid, but I smelled cop from him. So I wasn't sure. You know, if Lucinda's doing heavy lines, how can I trust her with the ice? Barnes left for Montreal this morning, and he's incommunicado. So I tried to reach you. I left a message on your cell phone."

Romy dials his cell phone and hears Pat whispering:

"Romy, it's Pat. Look, Romy, I'm here with Lucinda, man. She looks like she's been popping. There's some straight cat in a suit that's too big for him. They're at the bar. She says you know him ... and she's got the deal going down. But Barnes said nothing about this ... just the girl, Lucinda, man. So I'm like feeling squeezed. Please get back to me. My life may depend on it."

Romy puts the phone away and grabs Pat by the crotch, his fingers clenched at the scrotum. "Barnes said you'd deliver to me in the parking lot. You know the one."

Pat howls and bends over in pain as Romy lets go with a yank.

"Yeah, I been there a few times. I saw you there once."

"I was waiting two hours. Two fucking hours in the parking lot while you're downtown with the whore and her new pimp."

"You know him?"

Romy smacks his fist into his hand. "Yeah, I know him. His name is Parker, but the girls on the strip call him Pecker."

Pat wonders if Barnes may have set him up. "I don't know Barnes that well. When Jules was busted, I was out of a job. So

Barnes approached me with an offer. You remember, I asked you about him then, and – "

"I said he was cool. Barnes also asked about you."

"Look, Romy, I'm just a runner. That's all the heat I can take. I don't mess with guys like you, or Barnes – "

"Barnes! Lucinda must've got to Barnes and suggested this. He has a weakness for her. She worked for him out of Montreal. That's how I met Lucinda. At the time, I could see that Barnes really loved her. He didn't want her hooking. Apparently she looks a lot like his daughter who was killed in a three-car crash on the 401. But Lucinda met a cat named François who introduced her to his business friends. Only some of his friends were in politics, if you catch my drift."

"Yeah, but I'm not going there."

"Anyway, Barnes has friends in high places. Lucinda knew too much, so some local boys visit François in his boudoir and deliver the message. They were decent enough to call an ambulance. The next day, Barnes reaches me and says, 'I have this sweet kid. She's blonde ... she's eighteen ... she'll look good on your arm.' Barnes knows my clients are doctors, lawyers ... professional people. So Lucinda is a rave, but she is going overboard on the crack. I can't control her. I kicked her out of my stable when I caught her shorting me. I kept that from Barnes because he's always asking me how she is. So I say she's cool, she's happy ... you know, she's fine."

"You said this out of concern for how Barnes felt about her."

"No, out of concern he don't put me in traction. I have to reach Barnes before I take any action on Pecker."

Pat knows Romy has killed people for professional and personal reasons. "What about Lucinda? What happens to – "

"If I touch her, I may as well book into the morgue. She's out of control, and I can't believe Pecker is connected to Barnes. He's too low-life for Barnes. He's selling jumbos to kids on the street. I don't agree with selling crack to kids. I got a brother, twelve, and a sister, fourteen. I'm putting them both through school like I never had the chance to do. Sure, Lucinda was doing lines when she was with me, but I kept it under control for as long as I could. Pecker 's a junky. He's into Big Harry big time. He must have her on it too. My Detroit friends call that murder one ... H and coke."

"Oh, shit. Maybe that's what Lucinda was on at the bar."

"It's no good when your pimp is a junky, man. Me, I'm just a mouth worker. None of that needle shit for me. And Pecker has Lucinda doing cheap tricks on the strip so he can flag and fly first class. It's a shame with her looks ... and that great ass. Lucinda made a lot of money for me. But she was a bad influence on my other girls."

Romy's phone rings and he reaches into his jacket. "Yes, Mr. Elliot. I'm here with the Irishman. Yes, I know that went down. No, I didn't hear about ... When did it happen? That's a fucking shame. Uh huh. Okay. I'll bring him over. Sure. Ciao."

18:23

ROMY TAKES Pat by the arm and leads him to the street where a blue Mercedes is parked at the corner.

"Where we going, Romy?"

"I want you to meet somebody special."

Romy turns on the radio.

"Who is it, Romy?"

"Shhh," Romy raises the volume on a news report:

> The man found dead in the trunk of a car at Montreal Dorval International Airport this morning has been identified as prominent businessman Brian Barnes.

Pat turns to Romy. "Barnes is dead!"

"Shhh."

> In others news, the Prime Minister is reportedly considering the Opposition's demand for the resignation of two cabinet

ministers. In Parliament today, the Prime Minister was once again under siege:

Leader of the Opposition: I want the Prime Minister to come clean and tell the Canadian people why ... why, Mr. Prime Minister, were two of your cabinet ministers negotiating government contracts with known mob figures.

Prime Minister: (To jeers from the opposition). Mr. Speaker, I would like to answer the honourable minister's question if I am permitted to ... (more jeers). Mr. Speaker!

Speaker of the House: Order, please! Order!

Prime Minister: Thank you, Mr. Speaker. I too believe the Canadian people deserve to know what is at the bottom of these rumours and allegations. But I am not prepared to condemn anyone until we receive a full report from the RCMP to determine if an investigation is necessary.

(Howls of laughter from the Opposition)

A Member of the Opposition: Mr. Prime Minister, perhaps the RCMP will have their report written by the Disney Studios. After all, you are beginning to look more like Pinocchio every day.

(Pandemonium)

Romy switches off the radio and turns to Pat. "With Barnes out of the way, we can breathe easy."

"We? Who do you mean, Romy?"

Romy turns a corner onto a sidestreet.

"You'll see."

23:17

PAT LOOKS out the window at the slum houses: garbage on the sidewalks, stores with bars on their windows, kids playing ball hockey on the road, teens loitering outside a poolhall, aging hookers approaching cars, men who stagger out of the local tavern, people huddled in doorways with their belongings in bags. Pat wonders how it came to this for him? Being a mule for drug dealers when he doesn't even smoke. Being from Willowdale, the pristine suburbs where poverty is an abstraction and hard times is having to clean the pool once a week. Having a college education that qualifies him to say he has a college education. Taking heavy risks with the law, and heavier ones with gangsters like Romy. He glances at himself in the mirror, and the dark lenses looking back don't know him.

Romy parks next to a three-storey redbrick rooming house with people sitting on the steps. "Take those off."

"What?"

"The shades. Take them off. Mr. Elliot likes to see people's eyes when he talks to them."

Pat removes his sunglasses and leaves them on the dashboard. He follows Romy up the steps to where a group of people are sitting. An old woman shields her eyes from the sun to look up at him. A scrawny old man with a cane stands and Romy embraces him.

"Hello Mr. Elliot."

Peter Elliot admires Romy's Italian silk suit. "Roman, you are looking decidedly urbane in your sartorial splendour."

Romy laughs to keep from blushing, and explains to Pat: "Mr. Elliot never says five words when he can say ten."

"And your choice of vehicle, Roman, is another feature which must attract you to the law profession for reasons undesirable, hmmm."

"The cops like my taste. What can I say?"

"And who is your friend, Roman?"

"Mr. Elliot, this is Pat … uh, I don't know his last name."

Peter Elliot smiles: "Patrick Monoghan. Age 31. Graduated from Western University with a B.A, in Philosophy. A modest education, but not so immodest pursuit of wealth. Your most recent bank statement explains why you are here, Mr. Monoghan."

Pat feels sweat trickling down the curve of his back: "I save everything I earn, Mr. Elliot. I feel I deserve it for the risks I take every day."

Pat follows Romy and the old man into the dingy building and up a flight of stairs.

"You won't get rich from saving in a bank account, Mr. Monoghan. You need to invest. I will have Roman advise you on some wise investments."

26:21

INSIDE PETER Elliot's apartment, Pat's eyes take a few minutes to adjust to the dim lighting. He is surprised at how modestly Peter Elliot lives. Has he taken a vow of poverty? Either that or he is hiding from the law, or his past.

"Mr. Monoghan – "

"Excuse me, sir, I prefer to be called Pat ... I ... just prefer it, if you don't mind."

Well, with that settled, we shall all address each other on a first-name basis. In that case, Pat, please call me Peter."

Peter Elliot turns to Romy, who says, "Mr. Elliot, I can't ... uh, call you by your first name. Please, I feel it would be disrespectful."

Pat nods. "I agree, Mr. Elliot. I'm just Pat. Romy's Romy, or, as you say, Roman. And you're Mr. Elliot."

Peter Elliot leans forward, his piercing blue eyes fixing on Pat. "Pat, I understand you are clean."

"Yes, sir, Mr. Elliot."

"Good, I have no respect for drug addicts. They are the lowest form of vermin on the planet. But that is no reason to deny them their heroin, and their cocaine, and a whole array of chemical stimulants."

"The law would disagree, Mr. Elliot."

"Pat, do you know who all those people in prison are? You shrug, Pat, but I think you must know."

"They're lawbreakers like me who have been caught and imprisoned."

"You are a lawbreaker, Pat. But you are not in prison,"

"No, but I could be. They know about me."

"Ah, indeed they do. And they are familiar with Roman who

insists on flaunting his, shall we say, rather dubious lifestyle in a manner befitting a pimp."

"Hey, I'm proud to be a pimp."

"But there is one important difference between criminals like you and Roman and those who have been incarcerated."

"Well, they're in prison, and Romy and I aren't."

"That's correct. But why do you suppose that is?"

"Luck. I've been lucky."

Peter Elliot turns to Romy. "Why do you suppose that is, Roman?"

"I don't suppose, Mr. Elliot. I know why."

"Then would you please explain to Pat."

"Mr. Elliot, despite his modest appearance, is more powerful than the law. He protected Barnes until Barnes opened his mouth to too many people, including Lucinda."

Peter Elliot shrugs. "Yes, unfortunately, that ended our long and amicable association. So I am sad about the loss of your former employer, Pat. But life goes on. Roman's prostitution ring is a front for extorting businessmen. Thankfully, Roman seldom finds it necessary to use muscle. We have friends in law enforcement that look after such matters. He will, however, need to silence two misbegotten strays."

Pat turns to Romy, "Lucinda and her pimp?"

"Yeah, Pecker is feeding leads he gets from Lucinda to some smart ass young lawyer with political ambitions. I figure she's giving Pecker information a bit at a time, holding on so she can get the dope she needs. But she's self-destructive. So she knows where it's leading."

"One vindictive woman can destroy what many strong men have built. What Barnes confided to Lucinda, she has told to her pimp. It leads to places so high one could get giddy imagining it. So we won't imagine it, Pat. We will cut off the lines of communication. We will kill the messengers."

Pat would like to know why a man with Peter Elliot's power chooses to live like a pensioner in a slum neighbourhood.

"Pat, you are probably curious about why I live in these modest circumstances. Roman, would you explain to Pat?"

"Peter Elliot was once a powerful political figure. Although he was ruthless, he had the kind of charisma and connections that would have taken him to the highest office in the land. But destiny intervened."

"Not destiny, Roman. Fate. Remember, I possessed the opportunity to change my fate. Destiny cannot be changed. Fate can."

"Fate intervened, and Mr. Elliot's one human flaw led to political misfortune."

"Yes, my former wife."

Romy continues: "She was a younger woman. Very beautiful. Mr. Elliot returned from a political campaign to find her in bed with a man."

"Yes, a reporter who unfortunately met with an untimely death. A boating accident, I believe."

"There were others having flings with Mrs. Elliot."

"Yes, a promising young concert pianist whose musical career ended in misfortune when he had his hand crushed in the door of a limousine that was to take him to the airport. It took him to the hospital instead."

"The final blow was —"

"A poor choice of words, Roman."

"Uh … when Mr. Elliot learned his wife was having an affair with a political rival."

"That crushed me. I have had no desire for anything other than power since then."

"Mr. Elliot left politics and traveled the world for five years."

"For the first year, I lived rather comfortably, staying in the finest hotels. Then one day, while travelling through China, I met a young boy with a fishing pole sitting on the bank of a river next to a bridge. I speak Cantonese, so I stopped to talk to him. What he told me changed my life. His parents were killed in a hurricane that destroyed their village. Only a few people survived. At first he felt guilty about surviving while his parents and others perished, but this is what he told me he learned from the experience. 'It is my fate to be poor, but I will change that. Because I know it is not my destiny.' The boy pointed to people working in the fields. 'That is their destiny. But I will leave this country one day and they will stay to work the fields,' he said as he cast his line into the water. That boy came from a small impoverished village in China. He had lost his parents through no fault of his own. I was born into wealth. I never had to work as ordinary people work. Yet, as a politician, I promised so much to ordinary people ... the middle class ... the working class ... the poor. And it was all lies. I was only serving my class."

Pat realizes that Romy and Peter Elliot have divulged a great deal of information to him. Some of it may be fiction, but he knows there is also fact. He has come this far, but must take it one step further.

"Who are you serving now, Mr. Elliot?"

"Good question, Pat. To answer that I must first ask why you are in this racket? You came from a good home, good parents. You were never deprived. So tell me, why are you here, Patrick Monoghan?"

"Money. I'm in it strictly for the money. I don't understand the point of having power without wealth."

"Wealth means nothing to me, Pat. I choose to live modestly. But I realize it means a great deal to Roman and you, and to that boy from China who is now a man and owns a chain of motels across Canada. You see, it was his destiny to meet me, and mine to meet him. I can make people and break them, but I can't change the political system. I had hoped for better things when I returned from China. I wanted to resume my political career in Canada and somehow make amends for lying to the people who had supported me. But the press ridiculed me, and my former political associates destroyed whatever political aspirations I had."

Pat doesn't follow politics, and Peter Elliot's political past means nothing to him. "So you are one man against the political system that destroyed you."

Peter Elliot shrugs. "You are probing, Pat. You ask who I am serving, and want to know if I am one man against my political enemies. Well, quite frankly, I am not. There are others. You won't tell anyone, will you?"

Pat feels himself involuntarily squirming as he stands, hoping to leave.

"No, of course not."

"Would you like me to divulge names, Pat? Would that interest you? I understand there are listening devices about the size of a postage stamp that record with flawless perfection."

Romy smiles. "Digital micro recorders, Mr. Elliot."

Pat realizes Steve Petropolis had set him up. Petropolis must work for Mr. Elliot. He is either a crooked cop, or someone who led him to believe he was a detective working undercover. They arranged to meet in a shopping center parking lot, and Petropolis convinced him to wear the device. Pat backs toward the door, but Romy intercepts him.

Peter Elliot stands and leans on his cane. "I have a name for you, Pat. It's Petropolis. It's a phony name. But I don't suppose that matters now. Take Pat for a ride, Romy. I don't want a mess in my living quarters –"

38:14

Something Other Than Olives

"What's wrong with olives?" he asks her.

Sally plucks a black olive out of her salad and drops it deftly into his bowl. "Todd, you know I don't like their bitter taste."

"But it's not a Greek salad without olives. Olives are essential."

She lifts a piece of cucumber and finds another olive. "How many did you put in here?"

Todd reaches for her bowl. "Give me the damn salad. I'll get them out."

Sally pushes his hand away. "It's okay … I'll do it myself. That way I'll know they're all gone."

Todd promises himself he will never make another Greek salad for her. He had already compromised by using bland Canadian feta cheese rather than Greek because, she says, "Greek feta is too salty."

And, of course, she always cautions him about using too much garlic.

"Todd," Sally says with an olive stuck to the end of her fork. "Is it too difficult to put the olives in your bowl after the salad is served?"

Todd has given up trying to explain that the olives must be tossed with the salad for the flavour to be right. "But I thought I got them all out."

"There were five olives in my salad. How many did you get out?"

Todd tries to remember. "I think … Uh, about seven."

"About seven!"

"I remember there were seven because I counted them out loud."

"Well, learn how to count past seven," Sally shouts.

Todd knows that something other than olives is bothering her. "Why don't we just lay it out on the table … Right here. Let's discuss what's really bugging you."

"What do you mean?"

"It's more than the olives. There's something else bugging you."

Sally bites into a piece of cucumber.

"So what is it?"

"It's just the olives."

"No, it isn't. It isn't just the olives."

"Yes, it is."

"It can't be."

"Todd, it is the olives."

"C'mon, nobody gets angry over olives, Sally."

"I do when you put them in my salad … when you know I don't like them. Do you do it on purpose?"

Todd thinks the olives are an excuse for Sally to vent her frustration. "It's not good to keep it bottled up," he tells her

Sally crunches on a green onion.

"Spit it out, Sal –"

Sally drops her fork into the bowl. "Don't call me Sal. You know I hate being called Sal."

"Yeah, because you don't like to be reminded about who used to call you Sal."

"That was fifteen years ago, Todd. Why are you bringing Ron up over dinner?"

"You still love him, don't you?"

"Look, I had forgotten all about Ron until you raised the subject. Obviously, you haven't."

"Why should I forget about him? We were good friends. I have no reason to forget Ron."

"Let's just drop it."

"Okay, we'll drop it."

Sally pushes her chair back and it scrapes against the floor as she stands to leave the table: "You started this by calling me Sal when you know goddamn well that's what Ron always called me. You're just being an insensitive prick again."

Sally is right, Todd thinks. It was callous of him to bring Ron into their argument over olives. He is sure she still loves Ron, but that's no reason for him to hurt her over it. "I'm sorry, Sally, we shouldn't bash each other like this. Why do we do it?"

Sally kisses his cheek. "A good argument clears the air."

"I know. But when we argue over something like olives, we should stick to olives, and not dredge up the past. The past doesn't belong at the dinner table."

Sally sits back at the table to finish her salad. "That's right. After all, I've never thrown Myra up at you."

"Who?"

"Myra. Don't tell me you've forgotten who she is."

Todd's mind flashes back fifteen years to a dimly lit Greek cafe. He and Myra are eating Greek salads:

"I love Kalamata black olives," Myra says and Todd is impressed that she knows the name of the olives. He follows her eyes to the unlit candle on the table, and he fumbles in his pocket for a match.

"Usually the waiter lights it," Todd explains as he empties his pockets onto the table and sorts through scraps of paper and assorted debris looking for the matchbook he knows he has.

"It's all right," Myra says.

"No, it's not all right, Myra. How can we see our olives in the dark?"

Todd finds the matchbook and holds them up just as the waiter lights their candle. "Oh, thank you," he says.

Todd asks, "Did you know they rub the salad bowl with garlic?"

Myra nods, savouring the lemon and garlic flavour: "Mmmm, I can't believe how wonderful this is."

"Myra, do you know what they put in here?"

She pokes her fork around in the bowl: "Uh, there's endive and ... are those radishes?"

"That's right ... endive, radishes, green onions, shredded carrot, chick peas -"

"Chick peas!"

"Sure. Why? Is something wrong?"

She slides the bowl away and clutches at her throat: "You mean I was eating chick peas?"

"Sure," he says, holding a chick pea at the end of his fork.

"I hate chick peas," she tells him.

"Hate chick peas! How can anyone hate chick peas, Myra? I mean, they're so innocuous."

"So why did you marry me if you had more in common with Myra?" Sally asks.

Todd finishes chewing on a cucumber and says, "Because you love chick peas."

The Avenging Angel

O N HIS stomach on the gravel roof, shivering. Overhead, cold clouds in a chaotic dawn. The frenzied dark has blurred to grey in first light. The city below is close to waking. He rolls over on his back with the gun cradled in both hands and listens to himself breathing. A gust of wind almost rolls him onto his stomach again. The gun slips from his hands as he digs his fingers into the gravel and holds on. He listens to a siren shrieking, and he shrieks back. The siren fades but his throat still shrieks. It is the only sound he can make. He has given up trying to talk. Words have left him bleeding like raw meat on the street. But all that will change today.

A helicopter passes overhead. He lifts his automatic and pre-tends to shoot, but does not want to waste bullets. He will need them for the people who don't know him, don't want to know him. He feels the extra ammunition clips in his pocket, squeezes them. Enough to wound and kill a dozen people.

He has shaved his whole body for the occasion – head, face, legs, chest and genitals. A mass-murderer needs a new identity. He has given up his name to the avenging angel. He has shaved it from his memory, pulled out the roots of who he was so it will never grow back again. It was easy. Nobody can shit on his name anymore. He is invisible beneath the smokestacks and high rises towering above.

A swarm of pigeons swoops down on the roof. He shrieks at them and they fly off. He rolls over and crawls on his stomach to the edge of the roof. He counts one, two, three, four, five people on the sidewalks below. Not enough for a bloodbath. It's still too early. He checks his watch – 5:47 a.m. He can be patient. He has been waiting for this all of his life.

He rolls onto his back and looks up at the sun breaking through smog and clouds, on its way into a bloody morning. There will be a shoot-out. He will not surrender to the cops. He will not hurl himself to death from the roof. They will have to come after him and take their chances. He looks forward to killing and being killed.

He unzips his pants and starts pulling on himself. It may be his last, and he wants it to be good. It feels almost as warm as the gun in his hand. At first, he is tender with himself. He is gentle and his fingers work slowly. He loses himself in the rhythm playing easy beats in his groin. A motorcycle guns its motor below and the storm grows, the storm and the wind blasting across the roof, the early blast of traffic, brakes squealing, his hand in a rush, finger-nails digging in, voices echoing around him as if he were in a canyon, deep down, almost to hell and burning with rage to come, to kill, to get the bloodying over with, the semen crying, ejaculating the parents he could never love, touch, hold, be held by, one long blast that ends too soon and leaves him gasping.

People will think it's because he's from a broken home: rape, incest, brutality, love gone wrong. He's heard it all. "Your parents abused you." People will overlook evil, thinking there must be a more rational explanation.

He zips up and wipes his hand on his pants. Music from a car below blasts around him. The music tapers off into the clamour below but he keeps the beat going in his head until voices and traffic swallow it up. He checks his watch – 6:21 a.m.

He crawls back to the edge of the building and looks down at human clumps. He sees people at the corner waiting for the light to change. He will fire into the group. Drawing his arm forward, he takes aim. The light changes and the group disperses. "Fuck!"

People gather at the opposite corner where the light is red. He aims and fires and the light turns green and they scatter across the street. "You bastards!" he screams. He scans the street and sees a group clustered around a bus stop directly below him. He pants in anticipation. Aiming, he fires and hears a sharp metallic sound piercing the air. He fires again and sees chips of concrete blasting up from the sidewalk. Someone points up at him and people scatter. He stands and fires at everyone in sight. The wind slams against his back as he reloads.

He needs to hit someone in the head, chest, back, anywhere on the body. Hit one person, then another. Don't try and kill everyone all at once. That was a mistake. He picks one out, a man cowering in a doorway. He raises his arm, takes aim and is thrown to the gravel. His arms are twisted back. There are knees in his ribs, guns in his face. He tries to kick and punch, but he can only shriek. Five cops in flak jackets hold him down. He spits at them, and feels a fist crashing into his head.

HE WAKES up after a long, bad dream and wishes he could go back to sleep. In isolation. In a cell. Strapped down. In the morning, they will read him his rights. A lawyer will argue that he's crazy, and a psychiatrist will confirm psychosis. But he knows nobody will kill him. They don't have the guts.

Taking the Snake

THE ANTIQUATED air-conditioner bolted to the window rasps like an old man having an asthma attack. The bare bulb on the apple-green ceiling flickers. A seam in the faded rose wallpaper above the bed where he sits has peeled back, and the plaster beneath is water-stained. The young woman on the chair across from him unbuttons her blouse. She is chewing gum. He hears it clicking in her mouth.

"What'd you say you want?" she asks.

He wipes his sweaty forehead with a handkerchief. Even the air around him perspires. "I don't know."

She turns to hang her blouse on the chair and wonders if she heard right. "Did you say you don't know?"

He stares at the dusty blades whirring in the brown metal air-conditioner and nods.

She wonders what kind of freak she hustled up to this room. "You paid me enough for a fuck. You wanna fuck? A blow? What?"

He looks at the young woman unfastening her bra. She has a tattoo of a serpent on her left arm. "You're really a pretty girl, you know. What's your name?"

She tries to remember the last time anyone called her pretty and thinks back to elementary school. "Why you wanna know my name?

He looks away at the seam in the wallpaper. "I just asked."

She has used five different names in her business. Charlena is her favourite. Most of her customers use false names. One actually said his name was "John." "My name's Charlena. What's yours?"

He looks at her. "Me?"

Charlena slips out of her black leather skirt. "Yeah, you! What's your name?"

"Perry."

"I met a lotta guys, but nobody named Perry. It's an unusual name. I mean, it's different."

"Yeah," Perry laughs nervously. "So's Charlena. I remember an old song called *Charlena*."

"The only guy I heard with your name is Perry Mason."

"I don't like my name. Do you?"

"You mean do I like my name? Do I like Charlena?"

"No, your name is beautiful. You are beautiful. But my name … Forget it."

Stripped down, Charlena approaches the bed with a condom in her hand. She stops, raises his chin with her finger and says, "You know what you want now?"

Perry looks into her face and sees a child under the paint. "Jesus, you're so young. How old are you?"

Charlena turns away. "What the fuck is this … an interview?"

"I'm sorry."

"I'm eighteen, and I been hustling on the strip for two years. I never met a straight guy yet that didn't wanna fuck me. I met some that couldn't get it up. Is that your problem? How old are you, anyway?"

Perry hears people groaning in the room next door and footsteps in the hall outside. "I'm … I'm forty-one … and I'm married to someone I don't know. You know what I mean?"

Charlena's father turned forty last month. There was a big family celebration, but nobody invited her. She called him on the phone to wish him a happy birthday, but he hung up in her ear. She stood in the phone booth for what seemed like an hour with the sounds of familiar family voices and laughter still echoing in her ears. Her pimp, Jody, finally opened the door, saw her crying and held her. "It's okay, baby. We get stoned tonight after you score. Then it won't hurt no more." She woke up two days later, her arms and legs tied to a stranger's bed. She closed her eyes and waited until the stranger was done with her. "Yeah, I know what you mean," she tells Perry.

"My wife and I never talk. There's no love."

"If that's what you want, you're in the wrong room. I'm not your wife. I'm a hooker."

"No, you're a person."

"Fuck you, I'm a hooker, and your time is up. The Chinaman only rented this room to you for an hour. He'll be knocking on the door soon."

"I gave him money for two hours."

"You did!"

"I thought we could —"

"What! Talk more shit like we been doing. You better pay me for another hour," Charlena says as she holds out her hand.

Perry stands and removes a wallet from his back pocket. He unfolds a wad of bills and hands her five twenties.

Charlena snatches it from him, counts and stuffs it into her purse. "Look, if you have a problem with fucking, I'll blow you. You want me to blow you?"

"That wouldn't be right," Perry says.

"What's fucking right or wrong? That's just shit made up by people who wanna control our lives. There ain't no right or wrong. No rules."

Perry nods. "We're really all alone out here, aren't we?"

"Fucking right we're alone."

"And there are no angels ... I mean, nobody we can believe in."

"We're all taking it up the ass."

"Charlena, you really have it figured out. You know, I've studied the philosophies and mythologies of the world. I've read the masters of the language. I'm familiar with the spiritual teachings of great prophets. I've done all of this learning, but here I am with you in a cheap room on the strip."

"So what good has it done you, huh? You wind up with a soft dick, a broken heart, and a hundred-dollar hooker."

"What can I do about it?"

Charlena dresses. "You wanna get stoned with me?"

"Sure," Perry says.

"You mean it!"

"Sure," Perry says as he puts on his suit jacket. "But not here, and not the drugs they sell on the strip."

"What then?"

"Mescaline."

Charlena laughs. "Are you serious?"

"My wife left me for her tennis instructor. She walked out on all of this. My daughters are in college. I'm alone, and feeling abandoned."

"Not anymore you aren't," she says as she takes his arm.

STANDING AT the French door that looks out on a lavish garden and blue pool, he draws the hair back from her shoulders and kisses her neck. She feels his hands on her back. She turns to him and takes his hands into hers, kissing his palms.

He feels her tears filling his hands. He drinks from his palms until his lips are healed by the salt, and he kisses her on the mouth. "Who are you?" he asks.

She turns and walks away, but he is not anxious. He knows she is leaving to come back again. He opens the door and steps out into the garden, walking barefooted between the fire of red tulips and yellow day lilies on each side of the quarry stone path. White daisies splash their flames across his path. Sunflower embers burn bright holes in the sky.

A naked woman appears, but she is not Charlena from the strip. The paint is washed from her face. The tears are gone. Two hearts have replaced her eyes. "Who are you?" he asks.

"I'm you."

"You can't be me. I am me, and … I am you."

She laughs. "If you're me, you can't be Perry. You must have another name."

He nods toward the house. "You saw my name somewhere inside the house … Didn't you?"

"On an envelope, Mr. Charles Draper."

Charles Draper smiles, "I didn't realize I hated the name Perry until I made it up and then told you that's who I was. And you? What's your name?"

"Tanya."

"You just took off more than your clothes for me, Tanya."

Tanya tugs gently on his balls and feels them harden in her hand.

"So here we are stripped of pretence, innocents in the garden," Charles says.

"With nobody to love, but – "

"Each other."

Charles feels his cock rising in Tanya's hand. "Shall we leave the garden and take the snake with us?"

"If we don't, someone will kick us out."

Dragons Bring Rain

HENRY STEPS in out of the rain and folds his umbrella. The last of the lunchtime crowd straggles in twos and threes down the narrow stairs of the Golden Dragon. He leans against the wall, pops a fresh chicklet into his mouth and waits until each person passes.

Sung is reading the racing form at the bar when Henry approaches him and says "You have time for an old customer?"

Sung glances up over the top of his glasses and his face lights with recognition. "Chicklet! I thought you died and went to the race track in the sky."

"There've been days when I wish I had, Sung."

"Where've you been, Chicklet? I haven't seen you for at least two years."

"I've been doing a circuit of the U.S. tracks."

"All the big ones, huh?"

"Yeah, Pimlico, Belmont, Gulfstream, Hialeah."

"The last time I saw you was when you gave me the tip on Touch Gold in the Belmont Stakes. But you never came back to collect your commission."

Henry smiles, pops a Chicklet into his mouth and pats Sung on the shoulder. "I know."

"I'm sure you didn't return to Toronto for my soup. I owe you a grand."

Henry reaches inside his suit jacket and pulls out a notepad. He opens it on the counter and thumbs through some pages. "That's right, the 1997 Belmont Stakes. I gave you the tip and placed the bet with Vic. Vic said we were crazy betting against Silver Charm after it won the Preakness and Kentucky Derby. He thought it was a cinch for the Triple Crown. But I had some very reliable data come my way."

"I put your money away and haven't touched it since. You can collect before you leave."

"That's cool, Sung. Listen, I'm expecting two people. They'll be arriving at different times. But I'll be done with them no later than 4 p.m."

"No problem, the dinner crowd doesn't come in until after 5."

Sung calls a waiter, who leads Henry to his favourite table near the window overlooking Spadina Avenue. He orders brisket soup with noodles and a pot of Chinese tea. The neon dragon outside Sung's restaurant shimmers with yellow and red lights on the rainy window. Through the rivulets streaming on the glass, the traffic clogged along Spadina takes the shape of sinewy rain serpents with metallic scales. The waiter returns with a pot of tea, and a few minutes later Henry fills his cup. The soup arrives steaming to the table and the scent intoxicates him.

Henry finishes his soup and goes to the washroom to brush his teeth. In the mirror, he notices the grey at his temples. He thinks it ages him at least five years, but otherwise adds sophistication. Henry is happy with the texture and tautness of his skin, the absence of wrinkles or shadows under his eyes. His good looks, charm and confident gait still turn heads. Although he has never read anything deeper than a racing form, through his extensive experience with people from all walks of life, Henry's vocabulary is rich and varied. He is especially adept at remembering the pet phrases people use, and repeating them back to establish familiarity, inspire trust in whatever he is proposing. That includes marriage. It scares Henry to think that Nina might hear he is back in town. It scares him because he knows how often he is attracted to what he fears. Whenever he needed her, Nina had been there for him. Invariably on those occasions, he proposed to her and she started to make plans for a wedding. It bothered him to have conned her so often because if he ever acquired the itch to settle down, Nina, or someone like her, would be the woman. Henry notices a blemish at the cleft of his chin. This should not happen with the skin cleansers, toners and moisturizers he applies each day. He sighs at his otherwise perfect face, pops a chicklet and leaves the washroom.

A tall heavy-set man in a navy blue suit is sitting at his table. He stands when Henry approaches. "Mr. Taggart?"

Henry nods. "Just call me Henry."

"My name is Bernard Rose. My clients and friends call me Rosey."

Henry laughs when he notices a white rose in Rosey's lapel. "So that explains your boutonnière."

"I wear a fresh one every day."

The waiter arrives with two double Jack Daniels. The two men click glasses, sip and settle back in their chairs. "I understand you're a bourbon drinker, Henry. So am I."

Henry resists telling Rosey that Jack Daniels is not real bourbon. "It's as good as anywhere to begin."

"Indeed, our mutual friend is paying for my time here … so just start at the beginning."

Henry clears his throat. "It happened two years ago. At Christmas time. I had just come out of Lichtman's where I bought a racing form, and I run into a boyhood friend, Shaky."

"Henry Corson."

"You know him?"

Rosey nods. "I helped him beat a statutory rape charge."

"Anyway, Shaky tells me he's planning to buy an engagement ring for his sweetie."

"'C'mon, Chicklet,' Shaky says, 'I could use your advice. You got better taste than me.'

I ask Shaky how much he plans to spend but he does not answer. He says he saw some beautiful rings at a jewelry shop in the mall, so I follow him inside. The mall is packed with Christmas shoppers. Shaky puts on his dark glasses and we walk toward the shop.

'What is it with the shades?' I ask him.

'I just feel more confident with these on,' he says.

This does not sound curious because Shaky has a long history of anti-social behaviour. So I shrug and follow him inside. While Shaky is talking to the jeweler at the back of the shop, I'm admiring a Rolex Daytona watch in the glass case and gasping at the price. Next thing I know, Shaky is flashing past me with a gun, and the jeweler is hollering 'Thief!' I hear an alarm and I'm out of there. The thieving little bastard, Shaky, still has those fast feet from when he was a booster and robbed trucks. But the quickest I ever move is one minute to post time. So I'm figuring they'll catch me and I'll do the rap for him. Every direction I move in, I see cops and security guards. I try to lose myself on the up escalator, squeezing between people clutching shopping bags and boxes. On every floor I see security guards. I get off on the fifth floor because it looks like the busiest. That's when I discover it's Toyland. Some parents and children are crowded around a Santa Claus. I mix with the crowd. There's a lady with a little girl, and I walk next to her to make it look like we're together. She thinks I'm a salesman and asks me where the Barbie Dolls are. I tell her it's not my department, but notice an aisle with Barbie Dolls and point it out. I have no idea of an escape route, and I'm floundering. I'm badly in need of a plan. I come on a hall and see a washroom. I go inside and am mopping the sweat from my forehead when I hear footsteps. I hide in the toilet stall and bend to look under the door to see if it's anyone in a uniform. I notice the high boots and red pants and open the door a crack to see Santa Claus. At last, an opportunity for escape. I come out of the toilet stall and give Santa a solid shot in the back of the head. He goes down and I drag him into the stall. He's a big guy, so his outfit fits right over my clothes. I glanced at the mirror on the way out of the washroom and knew I was the best-looking Santa they ever had, although the white beard needed a trim. I walk out into the store. And I'm about to step on the down escalator when a man with a sobbing little girl in tow approaches me and says, 'Santa ... could you help us out?'

'Santa's off duty,' I say.

The father pleads with me. 'Oh, please, my daughter is breaking her heart thinking she missed having her picture taken with you. We just arrived when you were going off duty.'

'Come back tomorrow,' I tell him.

But the father persists. 'Oh, you know what kids are like. They can't wait.'

I'm exasperated and about to say, 'Tough, she's out of luck', when a clerk approaches and says, 'Fred, it'll only take a few minutes. We have the camera set up.'

Meanwhile, I anticipate that the guy in the washroom is going to gain consciousness soon. So the clerk leads me up to Santa's chair and I lift the little girl onto my lap. Her freckled tear-streaked face looks up into mine and I expect her to tell me what she wants for Christmas. But she says, 'You're not the Santa I saw leave when we arrived. He was a fat Santa.'

Someone shouts, 'Smile at Santa.' But the little girl shakes her head and frowns.

'What's wrong, dear?' I hear the mother saying as I head toward the escalator.

I read in the paper the next day that the original Santa was out cold for a half-hour. I didn't know this as I made my way down the escalators, past cops and security guards. I am sure nobody saw me – and Shaky, wearing shades, looks like all kinds of people. So nobody can identify the thief and his accomplice. Shaky ends up with a nice little collection of diamond rings he sells to his fence. And I split town, broke after borrowing money from Nina to buy an airline ticket. Actually, she gave me the money to buy a wedding ring. But I had no interest in seeing the inside of another jewelry shop."

ROSEY ORDERS two more Jack Daniels. "I understand you returned to Toronto because of a picture in a Florida paper. A picture of you and the jockey Stoney Carrero."

"Right! I met Stoney at a restaurant I frequented in Little Havana in Miami. He was a waiter there. I usually came in with a racing form so naturally the subject turned to horses. He said his grandfather in Cuba taught him how to ride, and he always had this crazy dream about being a jockey. So I talked to some people and he got a shot at showing them his stuff. The rest is sports history."

"He's an amazing athlete."

"Anyway, Stoney is being interviewed by the press and he sees me going into the Turf Club. He calls me over and has them snap a picture of us with our arms around each other. It ends up on the front page of the sports section and a Canadian tourist sees it."

"Santa?"

"Yeah."

"Did he contact you there?"

"No, as it turns out Santa and his wife had a flight back to Toronto that day. But he traced me, got my number and called. Santa said he saw my face in the mirror as I came out of the stall and he would never forget it."

Rosey shakes his head. "Impossible to prove."

"Yeah, I know. Except the cops dusted the toilet stall. They got prints, but I have no record so that didn't go anywhere."

Rosey gulps on the Jack Daniels. "They'd still have those on file. So what is it? Is Santa extorting you?"

"Yeah, but he's in a hard way. His daughter has leukemia. He came out and told me if it weren't for this he'd turn me in. I had him checked out and what he says about his daughter is true."

"What's he want?"

"Ten grand. He needs it for medication."

"Pay him. I could get you off even if there are prints. But you don't need any heat in your occupation. You've thrived because you're clean. Our mutual friend wants it kept that way."

The mutual friend, a wealthy Canadian businessman with a gambling addiction, paid Henry for inside information from U.S. tracks. Henry had more contacts than a lens factory. Fronting as a freelance tipster, "Chicklet" became a familiar character at the tracks in his impeccable white suits, silk *charmeuse* ties and shoes you could shave your face in. He ingratiated himself to jockeys, trainers and even owners, and was so informed that often they would seek his advice. Henry smiles, "It's a good investment for the tips I feed him."

Henry checks his watch. "I'm expecting the guy in about ten minutes."

Rosey stands and pats Henry on the back. "I would also advise that Santa be warned about serious consequences if this is not the end of it. Medication for leukemia can be expensive."

Henry smiles. "I know where he lives and works."

"Tell me, Henry, does this have anything to do with how you feel about the kid?"

"No, I don't care about his kid."

Rosey leaves and a few minutes later, a man in faded jeans and a baseball jacket approaches the table. Henry recognizes him right away.

"Are you Henry Taggart?"

"That's right."

"I'm Fred Tanner."

The two men sit and Henry asks if he'd like a drink.

"No thank you. I don't want to prolong this."

"Okay, Mr. Tanner. So tell me how I can be sure that if I pay up, you won't continue to extort me, or eventually turn me in."

"You can't be sure. I can only give you my promise."

"Promise!" Henry laughs. "I'll tell you something, Mr. Tanner. If you ever did try to nail me for this, I have had legal advice that tells me I walk. Furthermore, if such ever happens nobody in your family is safe. I suspect you are a truthful man, but I'm not depending on it. It might help your conscience to know that

I was an innocent party in the jewelry store heist. It does mine. I am only guilty of stupidity."

Henry removes an envelope from inside his jacket. "Now you go into the washroom there and count it. I promise not to come in and knock you unconscious."

Fred returns a few minutes later, thanks Henry and leaves. The dinner crowd starts appearing and Sung approaches Henry, handing him an envelope and a box of chicklets. Henry says, "Lucky Eight in the fifth at Woodbine."

"Eight is the number for prosperity," Sung says. "Is it a cinch?"

"Nothing's a cinch, Sung."

The two men embrace and Henry leaves.

THE RAIN has stopped and Henry finds a telephone booth. "Hello, Nina. Yeah, it's Chicklet, honey. Look, I really missed you. I just had to come back to Toronto to see you. Sure, I'll get a cab and be right over."

Henry hails a cab on Spadina. He climbs in and it disappears into the traffic.

About the author

TED PLANTOS has published eleven collections of poetry, including *Mosquito Nirvana* (Wolsak and Wynn, 1993), *Dogs Know About Parades* (Black Moss Press, 1993), *Daybreak's Long Waking: Poems Selected and New* (Black Moss Press, 1997), and most recently *Five O'Clock Shadows* (Letters Bookshop), *Mix Six* (Mekler & Deahl), and *The Edges of Time* (Seraphim Editions).

He has also published two children's books, the acclaimed best-selling story *Heather Hits Her First Home Run* (Black Moss Press, 1986, also available on CD-ROM from Discus) and poems *At Home On Earth* (Black Moss Press, 1991).

His poems, short stories, articles and reviews have appeared in numerous magazines and anthologies, including: *Antigonish Review, Arc, Books in Canada, Canadian Author & Bookman, Canadian Forum, Canadian Literature, Dandelion, Exhibit B, Greenfield Review, Paragraph, Pittsburgh Quarterly, Saturday Night, Love and Hunger* (Aya Mercury, 1989), *Windfield Review, Windhorse Reader, Great Canadian Murder and Mystery Stories* (Quarry Press), *We Stand On Guard: Poems and Songs of Canadians in Battle* (Doubleday Canada).

He was the co-founder with Clifton Whiten of *Poetry Canada Review*. He was the founding publisher and editor of *Cross-Canada Writers' Magazine*, for ten years one of Canada's leading literary periodicals. In 1986, he founded the Milton Acorn Memorial People's Poetry Award. He is co-editor of *People's Poetry Letter*. He recently founded and edits *The Literary Network News*, an on-line international publication for writers.